Rabble Starkey

Rabble Starkey

LOIS LOWRY

Houghton Mifflin Company
Boston

Library of Congress Cataloging-in-Publication Data

Lowry, Lois.
  Rabble Starkey.

  SUMMARY: Many things change for twelve-year-old
Rabble Starkey, her mother, and her best friend,
Veronica Bigelow when Veronica's mother becomes
mentally incapacitated and the Starkeys move in
with the Bigelows.
  [1. Friendship—Fiction. 2. Mentally ill—Fiction.
3. Mothers and daughters—Fiction] I. Title.
PZ7.L9673Rab 1987   [Fic]   86-27542
ISBN 0-395-43607-9

Printed in the United States of America

HAD 10 9 8

Rabble Starkey

1

Veronica looked over from her desk and whispered to me when she saw Mrs. Hindler go to the supply closet and take out construction paper.

"Family trees," Veronica whispered. "I bet you anything."

But it wasn't no big secret or surprise. All the girls around us was whispering the same thing: family trees.

You get decimals in sixth grade, at least in our school, at least in our town of Highriver. Decimals in Math, and in Geography, South America, with all the capitals and major products and names of mountains you can't spell or pronounce, not even if you practice at home and study.

And family trees. Family trees is something Mrs. Hindler done with the sixth grade at the beginning of every year, so me and Veronica knew it was coming.

Mrs. Hindler stood up in front of the class with a piece of construction paper all marked up so's it looked like an apple tree with people's names printed right inside the apples.

Then she showed us on the board, with chalk, how it worked. You put your own name in first, see, right in the middle apple, with your birthday printed in smaller, underneath. Then all your folks become apples on the limbs. Mrs. Hindler showed us how she had a brother named Ralph, and where she had written in his apple: Ralph Weaver (Weaver was her name, too, she said, before she got married to Mr. Hindler) and his birthday. Then, under that, it said "Dec."

"What does dec mean?" Roger Watkins called out. Old Roger, he always forgot to raise his hand, so's he seemed rude, but he really wasn't so bad.

Mrs. Hindler picked out the "Dec." with her long, pointy red fingernail and stood there looking mournful. "My brother Ralph has passed away," she said. "That's what it means."

"Oh," Roger said. "My grandpa is dec," he added. "I'll write that in under my grandpa's name."

Everybody started murmuring, thinking up who in their family was dec.

"It means 'deceased'," Mrs. Hindler explained. "It's an abbreviation for 'deceased'." But I don't think many people was listening. They was all still talking to each other about who they knew who was dec. I could hear old Norman Cox in the back row, saying his dog was dec. Norman Cox's dog was *double* dec, if you ask me, run over by both front and back wheels of the J. C. Penney's delivery truck last spring.

Leaving school that afternoon, me and Veronica, we was each carrying our piece of construction paper — mine was yellow, hers was blue — and thinking about our family trees. Letitia and Felicia Saunders came past us, laughing, and we laughed with them.

"You should've asked her for a whole *pack* of paper!" I called to them.

One of them — I never could tell which one, since they was identical twins and always dressed alike — called back, "Our tree won't have room for any leaves! Just nothing but apples!"

The Saunders was the richest black family in Highriver, and also the one with the most children. Mrs. Saunders, she had a baby every single year, and there was something like thirteen of them already. Letitia and Felicia always had their hair done up in them rows of fancy braids, and so did all their sisters. I could never figure out how their mother had time to braid all that hair. But maybe she had maids. Their daddy owned a big factory that made doorknobs and stuff, and they lived in an enormous house with religious statues in the yard. I always wanted to see the inside, but the twins, though they was friendly enough in school, never invited kids to their house. I suppose it was full enough already.

Veronica and me headed home. "I don't even have no sisters or brothers, not even any dec," I said, gloomy-like. "You got Gunther, at least. But my old apple will be all by itself there in the middle."

"Yes. I have Gunther. But Mrs. Hindler said we

3

could put cousins in, and I don't have a single cousin, Rabble. You told me you have a million cousins."

That cheered me up a little, when I remembered that cousins could be apples. "That's right, I do! Some dec, even. My cousin Liddie got herself killed one summer falling off a tractor. Course she shouldn't of been on a tractor at all, she was only about five years old, so her big brother got into lots of trouble for riding her with him."

"You can put 'dec' after her name," Veronica said, "and then write her brother's name in black ugly letters, since it was his fault."

"Yeah, I might." I thought about that, remembering my cousin Joth, a fat blond boy with pale blue eyes. After Liddie slipped off the tractor that summer, Joth always slunk around all furtive and scared-like, looking behind him now and then as if somebody might sneak up and get even.

"I don't even know nobody's last name, among my cousins," I confessed to Veronica. "I gotta ask Sweet-Ho tonight. I hope she remembers."

Veronica pushed her hair back out of her eyes and glared at her sheet of blue paper. "I know everybody's names," she said, "but I don't have very many. I'm going to have the barest, dumbest-looking tree in the sixth grade."

"You want some of my cousins?" I asked. "I don't need 'em all."

"Maybe. Let's do them together, tonight, so if we need to borrow back and forth, we can, okay?"

I nodded, even though I knew I didn't need to bor-

4

row none from Veronica, having so many of my own already. But it makes people feel better if you try to come out even. I wouldn't mind if she wanted to loan me Gunther for my tree, since I didn't have no brothers and I liked Gunther, having known him since the very day he came home from the hospital newly born, four years ago. "Gunther Philip Bigelow" could look pretty fine, printed all neatly inside of an apple. Mrs. Bigelow surely had some severe and worrisome problems, but she had a grand history of choosing names for her children. Veronica's middle name was Gwendolyn, and between her two names she had more syllables than anybody I knew.

We was just coming around the corner by the Bigelows' house when Norman Cox came by on his bike, heading home. We could see his family-tree piece of construction paper — his was green — sticking out of the notebook in his bike basket.

"Gonna work on your family tree full of rotten apples, Starkey-Parkey?" he yelled.

I ignored him mightily. I made a motion to my ear, like I was turning off my hearing aid. My Great Aunt Elna used to do that for real.

"How about you, Bigelow-Pigelow?" Norman yelled at Veronica. "Who you got on your tree, besides crazies?"

Veronica tossed her head, ignoring him same as me, but I could tell she was embarrassed. Norman skidded past us on his bike, up toward the Coxes' driveway. His rear wheel skittered some pebbles toward us, stinging our legs.

Usually I make a practice of making no reply to rudeness. But it overstepped the bounds of decency, what Norman said to Veronica, calling attention to certain family problems. I yelled after him finally. "At least Veronica and me don't got a father who wears a dress!" I yelled.

It wasn't fair, really, since Norman's father wore work pants just like everybody else's father, most of the time. He only wore that long dress at church on Sundays, like the rules said he should, and I couldn't really fault him none for that. But sometimes you just lose your common sense when you feel the need to yell something hurtful.

Norman only laughed a spiteful sort of laugh, and sped away, holding his middle finger right straight up in the air where everybody in the neighborhood could see it, even his own mother if she happened to be looking out the window.

Shoot, it wasn't even really my neighborhood, either, if you want the whole entire truth. Me and Sweet-Ho, we was just hired help at the Bigelows. We didn't own a house or even pay rent. We just lived in two-rooms-and-a-bath up over the Bigelows' garage and held our breath tight every time Mr. Bigelow idled his Plymouth so the fumes drifting up through the floor and seeping through our braided rug wouldn't knock us flat dead.

But Veronica was just my age, twelve, and so we was friends. The differences between her and me didn't matter. I didn't much care that she lived across the yard in that bedroom all ruffled up and fancy because, shoot, she didn't care about it and made fun of the ruffles herself. And I sure wasn't jealous that she was filling out and getting a womanly figure all of a sudden while I was still a skinny Minnie. Veronica herself hated the thought of it, and slept on her stomach without fail, trying to mash her chest in so's it would stay flat. Both of us knew that once you start getting a big womanly chest, that's when lifelong trouble and sorrow begins.

We knew that secondhand from observing Veronica's mother, whose life was crowded with trouble, *weighted down* with trouble, even though she pretended otherwise and always without no exceptions had a smile pasted on her lips, even when she slept. Veronica and me, we spied on her once for that very reason, and it was true, Mrs. Bigelow slept smiling, and that is one of the saddest things I have ever learned through spying.

Even more, we learned about womanly trouble and sorrow from Sweet-Ho, who sometimes would talk to us about it in the kitchen of the Bigelows' house after supper was done. Gunther, he'd be all put to bed by then; and Mrs. Bigelow, well, she'd be off by herself same as always, roaming about the house, touching things, smiling and smiling. And Mr. Bigelow would go back to the office.

Veronica and me would set in the kitchen watching Sweet-Ho clean up, sometimes helping her put things away, now and then picking at leftovers before they got sealed up. Then when she was done, Sweet-Ho would pour us all a glass of iced tea, and we'd set there at the table, Veronica with her arms folded across her chest to mash it in, Sweet-Ho with her shoes kicked off both to soothe her feet and also so's Veronica and me could admire her toenails, which she kept painted a deep, romantic crimson.

We'd coax her a little — Sweet-Ho liked to be coaxed. Then she'd tell about the trouble and sorrow that came to her once she filled out.

And Sweet-Ho, she knew for real, from experience. Shoot, she was only fourteen when she had me.

Veronica and me spread out our construction paper on the table and started to explain to Sweet-Ho about the trees.

But Veronica interrupted the explanation. She was still remembering what happened on the way home from school. "I sure do dislike Norman Cox, Sweet-Ho," she said. "He yells remarks."

"Me too," I said. "I hate Norman Cox more than anything."

"Did anybody ever yell remarks at you, Sweet-Ho, when you were twelve?" Veronica asked.

I settled back in my chair, even though it wasn't very comfortable, being wood, and me being bony. All of our talk about Norman Cox was just part of the coaxing so that me and Veronica could get Sweet-Ho to telling about her own past troubles, stories we'd heard a hundred times before. But so romantic and sad and sweet that Veronica and me, we got all choked up again and again, listening.

Sweet-Ho folded a dishtowel and hung it up to dry. She sat down with us at the table and ran her fingers through her long hair. "Starting when I was just about eleven or twelve," she said. "Remarks and more than remarks, sometimes. Grabbing at me if they thought nobody was looking."

Veronica wrapped her arms around herself, as if someone might grab. "What did you do?" she asked.

Sweet-Ho grinned. "I punched Tracker Stargill flat one time. Gave him a bloody nose."

"You hated Tracker Stargill," I pointed out, since I had heard the story so often before. "He had no brains. He was still in third grade when he was fifteen."

"Wonder what ever happened to Tracker Stargill," Sweet-Ho said suddenly, looking into the distance almost as if her memory might be back there, behind the kitchen range, maybe, or through the window. "He'd be thirty years old by now."

"Probably still in third grade," I hooted. "World record for number of years in third grade!"

"Tell about Ginger Starkey next," suggested Veronica. "Rabble and I have to work on these trees for school, but I want to hear about Ginger Starkey first."

"You pour the iced tea, Rabble, honey," Sweet-Ho said. I unwound my feet from the rungs of the chair

9

and went to the refrigerator. Sweet-Ho always needed something to sip before she talked about Ginger Starkey.

She cooled her hands around the glass when I brought it to her. Me and Veronica tasted ours and added sugar.

"He had that ginger-colored hair," Veronica said, prompting. "And he had already finished tenth grade several years before, and you were just in eighth." Sweet-Ho smiled. She has a wonderful smile, and she doesn't use it just any old time. Sweet-Ho's is an occasional, important smile, and she's never wasteful of it.

"He had that ginger-colored hair," Sweet-Ho began, "and it was the first thing I noticed about him when I saw him. It was a hot day, one of those days when the sun makes everything seem as if it's moving, you know? And you have to squinch your eyes up to slits, even just to see, because it's so bright — and lord, there was this bright ginger-colored hair, shimmering in that heat. And I didn't even see anything else at first, just that hair. He was sitting in the driver's side of a blue Ford pickup, parked in front of Appleby's General Store, and I had walked to Appleby's to get some — what was it, now? I forget."

"Molasses," Veronica and I said together.

"Right. Molasses, for my mother, because she needed it for the cinnamon cookies she was about to bake, and she thought she had some, but when she went to reach for it, it just wasn't there. She had a suspicion that Verna Cooper had come right into the house and borrowed it without asking when nobody

10

was home. Well, anyway, that must be fate, because if we hadn't needed molasses, and I hadn't gone down to Appleby's to get some at that exact moment —"

"— because the pickup was about to leave, right?"

"Right. Its engine was running, and Ginger Starkey was only just waiting for the fellow he was with, who was inside Appleby's buying some cigarillos. They were going to go to the stock-car races, Ginger and — I can't remember his name —"

"It don't matter. His name don't matter," I interrupted, knowing she would search and search for that name, but it would never be there.

"Then he saw you, and you saw him," Veronica said, all dramatic-like.

Sweet-Ho held the icy glass against her mouth. She licked its cold side. She smiled. "He saw me and I saw him, and that was it. I never even completed my errand before I was climbing into that truck and we exchanged a few smiles and a few words and then we was driving away and clean left his friend behind as well. And there I was only thirteen years old, and Ginger Starkey, he had finished tenth grade and been out of school for three years — he was probably twenty, even —"

"And you'd never been with a guy who drove his own pickup before, and next thing you knew —"

She took the story back from me. "Next thing I knew, we was already in the next county and I made him stop so's I could send a postcard to my mother."

"And the postcard said —" That was Veronica asking. Veronica always liked what that postcard said.

11

Sweet-Ho laughed. " 'Dear Mama, I have gone off to get married and I forgot your molasses. By the time you get this my name will be Sweet Hosanna Starkey.' "

"She forgave you, though," I said with satisfaction.

"She forgave me because I came home with a ginger-haired baby," Sweet-Ho said, "and my mama, she was a pushover for babies of any kind, and she'd never seen one with hair like that before." She reached over and ran her fingers down through my hair. "It's still just as pretty as your daddy's was, Rabble."

But I pulled away. I don't care none about having pretty hair. "Tell how she named me, too, Sweet-Ho."

"Well, I was just young and foolish, you know? And Ginger Starkey, he didn't care. I didn't know it, but by the time you was born he was already making his getaway plans. Lord, he'd probably pulled up that pickup beside some other little girl with eyes for ginger-colored hair. So when you came and I asked him what to name you, he didn't say nothing or indicate any interest, and me, all I could think of was movie star names, and I couldn't even choose one for all that. So you went a month with no name, and then another month with no name and no daddy to boot, because Ginger Starkey was gone by then. And then I got on a Greyhound and went back home, and first thing Mama said after she saw you was —"

Me and Veronica said it together: " 'Look at them sea green eyes. Look at that ginger-colored hair. Lord, lord, trouble lies ahead for this child.' "

"That's exactly what she said," Sweet-Ho went on.

12

"What did she mean, trouble?" I asked. "I never have no trouble."

Sweet-Ho grinned. "It was just her way of saying that you would grow up beautiful."

"So she gave me a Bible name."

"That's right. She said, " 'We'll stave off what trouble we can with a Bible name.' "

"Parable Ann Starkey," I announced with pride.

"I have more syllables," Veronica said. "But you, Rabble, you've got the more meaningful name. And you've got your daddy's pretty ginger-colored hair. And once you fill out, Rabble, then, sure as anything, you're going to have —"

"Trouble and sorrow," Sweet-Ho said, but she was laughing. "Come on, you two, let's get at those family trees or you'll both of you flunk sixth grade."

2

Shoot, Sweet-Ho, I don't have no brothers or sisters at all, just my one dumb apple sitting there all alone in the middle. I wish I could've been twins. Or that you and Ginger Starkey could've had one more baby. Or that you got married again, maybe, and —"

"Hush up, Parable. Don't ask for trouble," Sweet-Ho said, laughing.

"Anyway," Veronica said, trying to make me feel better, "I'm just putting Gunther in a little squinchy apple over here on the side, like on a twig, not a whole branch. See?"

I looked over at her family tree and saw what she meant: her brother's name was printed neatly on a little circle, nothing show-offy about it. Just "Gunther Philip Bigelow." And underneath, his birthday.

I started to laugh. "Remember old Gunther when he was first born, how homely he was?"

Sweet-Ho bit her lip. "Lord, lord," she said. "He was the homeliest thing I ever saw, bar none. I don't

14

mean any offense, Veronica, you know that, you know we all love Gunther."

But Veronica wasn't offended at all. "I always love homely things best," she said. "Kittens or puppies or anything, I always love the runt best. I don't care that Gunther's homely. And I know my daddy doesn't, my daddy thinks Gunther's just the best old thing ever. And he thinks that about me too, of course."

That was true. Mr. Bigelow loved both his kids more than anything.

"Look here, now, Sweet-Ho," I said. "I'm gonna put big swirly branches out here to both sides, for cousins. What's Liddie and Joth's last name? And tell me all the others, too. I'm gonna loan some to Veronica."

We bent over our papers, Veronica and me, drawing apple shapes on the branches, and Sweet-Ho gave us names to put in. Poor old dead Liddie — her whole name was Lydia Louise Jones, Dec., age five — I took her and her blameful brother Joth. But I gave Veronica some others that I didn't like much. Veronica got my cousins Marilyn Ann and Marissa, the ones with hair so yellow it was almost white, and their eyes were all pinkish, and their mama always made them wear those dumb old socks with lace around the edge. I hadn't seen them since I come to Highriver to live four years ago, but I was sure they was just the same, spiteful and mean-spirited with their rabbity faces. Veronica wanted them, anyway; she liked their fancy names.

Sweet-Ho couldn't remember anybody's birthdays

15

so we just put in the ages. Thirteen and fourteen, Marilyn Ann and Marissa would be, because they was a little older than me, so Veronica wrote that in.

I watched while Veronica printed in her mama's name real careful, and nobody, not me or Sweet-Ho or Veronica herself, said a word. Alice Mayhew Bigelow was the name of Veronica's mama.

And then, as if writing the name had made it happen, the door to the kitchen came open and Veronica's mama came walking in. It was her house, where she lived, of course, so no real surprise that she should be walking about the rooms in the evening. But somehow Mrs. Bigelow always came as a strange surprise anyway. And lately her strangeness had been getting worse.

She didn't say nothing, just walked through the kitchen, smiling real pretty. She looked down at the table where Veronica and me was working, but she didn't ask questions — you'd think she would ask questions, seeing those foolish trees and apples, and one of them with 'Alice Mayhew Bigelow' printed on it plain as anything. But she just walked past. She picked up a blue crayon off the table and held it in her hand, rubbing at it with her fingers, so that some of the blue came right off on her skin. She looked at that blue fingertip and smiled. Then she put the crayon into the pocket of her dress and went away.

"Good night, Mama," Veronica called after her, in a sweet voice. Her mama didn't answer and for a minute the kitchen was quiet.

"Now I'm going to do one for my grandma," I said,

to do away with the quiet because it was making me feel funny, the way I always felt when Mrs. Bigelow was around. Then I drew a nice round apple for my grandma, Sweet-Ho's mama, the one who gave me my name.

"How do I spell Gnomie, Sweet-Ho?" I asked. Gnomie was what we all called my grandma, and it always made me think of them painted clay creatures some people put in their yards, holding a fishline into a little pond, some of them, and wearing pointy hats. Gnomes. My grandma was little and squat, like them.

But Sweet-Ho spelled it out for me, and I was downright startled. It wasn't Gnomie at all. It was Naomi. All those years I had the thought wrong in my head.

I printed "Naomi Jones" in my grandma's apple, real careful. Under her name I printed in "Dec." Then I drew another special apple underneath.

" 'Sweet Hosanna Jones Starkey.' There you are, Sweet-Ho. See how I did that? Now look, how I draw a line over, joining you up to this apple here. This one's gonna be Ginger Starkey."

"He could be dec for all we know," Sweet-Ho commented.

Veronica looked up from her paper. "Of course he isn't," she said. "He's out seeking his fortune somewhere. Someday he'll come back. You just wait and see."

Sweet-Ho and I didn't say nothing to argue with her. Veronica was the nicest person we knew, and if she wanted to believe old Ginger Starkey would come back, that was okay. Me and Sweet-Ho knew better, though. We had talked about it lots, at night before we went to sleep, and we had decided long ago that we wouldn't be seeing Ginger Starkey again probably ever. Twelve years he'd been gone and no word. Sweet-Ho thought he might even be in Hollywood, with his name changed, he was that handsome; sometimes, she said, she watched all the unimportant characters in movies, thinking she might catch a glimpse of him.

Other times, she said he could be just a dumb old bum somewhere by now, maybe with all his teeth fallen out. But I don't think she believed that, and I know I didn't.

Sometimes me and Veronica, in thinking about things, used to wonder if Sweet-Ho ever got lonely for a man around. We asked her once, but she said no. She said she had some boyfriends now and then after I was born and she left me at my grandma's. She said she had some good times and all.

But then she got tired of it, and she missed me, she said, and finally Gnomie — I have to call her that still, because the thought was so strong all those years, I don't expect I will ever adjust to the startlement of it being wrong — died after being sick with poisonous kidneys for a while. So Sweet-Ho she came and got me and brought me here to the Bigelows' garage to live.

She'd been working as a waitress, see, down to Buddy Rivet's Seafood, and she'd met Mr. Bigelow, Veronica's father, there. His real estate office was

18

right there, downtown, and he used to come into Buddy Rivet's for lunch. Mr. Bigelow is the kind of man who takes an interest in people — all kinds of people — and he knew all the waitresses at Buddy Rivet's. He knew that Leona Harrison suffered from varicose veins and a husband with a fondness for drink. He knew that Carol Sue Brown had been Miss Elkins County in her prime a few years back, and now was selling Mary Kay products on the side, hoping to win a pink car.

And he knew that back with her family in Collyer's Run, Sweet Hosanna Starkey had a little girl named Parable Ann, the same age as his own little girl. Me and Veronica was both eight years old then.

It was right at the time that Mrs. Bigelow was expecting Gunther, though of course she didn't know it was Gunther she was expecting; it might have been just about anybody, but it turned out to be Gunther, the homeliest baby in Highriver, West Virginia, bar none.

And Mrs. Bigelow wasn't up to snuff. She'd been having a lot of these emotional problems for some time, see, and Mr. Bigelow was worried about would she be able to care for the new baby that was coming. So when Gunther was born, he hired Sweet-Ho to come there and help out, pointing out to her that it was a way she could have her little girl there with her, something that Sweet-Ho surely did appreciate.

While Mrs. Bigelow was still in the hospital, Sweet-Ho came to Collyer's Run to get me and we both showed up at the Bigelows' with everything we

19

owned in two suitcases with busted locks and a couple of giant trash bags, the four-ply kind you see in them commercials. Mr. Bigelow didn't blink an eye. He just said, "How do you do, Parable Ann," when we was introduced, and he said he had a little girl just my age and he would go to find her right that minute. Then he handed Sweet-Ho the scrawniest baby in the world, and it was Gunther, with his face all scrunched up homely and his little drumstick legs sticking out straight from them big diapers.

Veronica's mother, she had to stay in the hospital longer than Gunther, see, because she had all these emotional problems, which they was trying hard to fix. And also she was getting herself all sewn up shut so she wouldn't have no more babies. Anyone would do that if they gave birth to something as homely as Gunther, if you ask me, so I don't fault her none and neither does Veronica. What we can't figure out is how she ever goes to the bathroom, all sewn up shut as she is. But shoot, you can't ask somebody that, not somebody who smiles all the time but doesn't talk none, like Mrs. Bigelow, and who seems to have some kind of serious trouble going on.

Me and Sweet-Ho, we settled right in and been here ever since, right in two rooms up top of the garage. For a while, when he was a baby, Gunther, he lived here, too, even though he was technically a Bigelow.

"Rabble," Sweet-Ho said, that first day after she set that homely baby down on the drainboard of the sink and looked around. "Right here is what you and me is going to call home."

Now I'd been at my grandma's for all them eight years, excepting for the past few months when Gnomie had the poisonous kidneys, and I went round and stayed with cousins here and there. I never lived up over no garage before. But it didn't look too bad. Needed scrubbing, but shoot, I was good at that.

"We don't gotta keep that here with us, do we?" I asked Sweet-Ho, pointing at Gunther. He was sound asleep right there on the drainboard beside a can of Ajax. If we'd wanted to we could of shot him with the rubber squirting hose on the sink. I kind of wanted to, but I didn't say it.

"Shoot, no," Sweet-Ho said. "His mama'll be coming home any day now. We can stand him till then. And you like that girl okay, don't you?"

"Yeah." I had liked Veronica right off. She was kind of shy when her daddy introduced us, but she had piercy eyes and curly hair and I could see she was wearing a big diamond ring, the kind you get from a candy machine if you hit it just right.

"Which bed you want?" Sweet-Ho asked. There were two, side by side, metal frames sagging in the middle and smelling of mildew. One was by the window and I chose that.

Sweet-Ho had the one by the closet then, and she stuck some of her stuff on the wall there for decoration, using thumbtacks that we found in a drawer, and the heel of her waitress shoe for a hammer. She had a lot of leftover stuff they give her from Buddy Rivet's when she quit: IN GOD WE TRUST, ALL OTHERS PAY CASH, for one. TODAY'S SPECIAL: SALISBURY STEAK, $2.99, that was another, and to me it didn't make much sense to put that one on the wall of your home where you live. But Sweet-Ho liked it; she said it made her feel nice memories of her days at Buddy Rivet's, plus a certain satisfaction that she didn't have to be a waitress no more, even though the tips was good. And she had a poster of Willie Nelson in concert.

I didn't have nothing to stick up on the wall by my bed except a Mammoth Caves bumper sticker that my cousin traded me once for a Bible verse card I got at Sunday school. And I had a magazine picture of whales leaping up out of the sea, which I tore out of a magazine Sweet-Ho bought me to read on the bus when she brought me to Highriver. So I stuck that up, too. And after I shook the blankets outside they didn't smell so mildewy when I put them back on the beds. Sweet-Ho covered them each with one of the quilts that Gnomie had made.

About that time there was a funny sort of squealing noise from the sink in the kitchen, and at first Sweet-Ho and I thought, uh-oh, the plumbing's busted. But then we both remembered at about the same time. She went and picked up Gunther from the drainboard, and we noticed that when he was awake he was cross-eyed.

But when Sweet-Ho set down and started to feed him from the bottle Mr. Bigelow had left in the icebox, she said she kind of liked him, even in spite of his homeliness. Gunther, I mean. She set there in an old straggly wicker rocking chair that needed paint, and Gunther lay in her lap, just all relaxed and homely and cross-eyed and sucking away. And she said, "Parable Ann, I do believe I'm settling down for good. I believe this is all I need."

That made sense, because what you got to realize is that by then, with all the traveling around Sweet-Ho had done while I was with my grandma and all, a lot of years had passed and she was middle-aged, or at least almost. Twenty-two is what Sweet Hosanna Starkey was when she brought me to the Bigelows' garage to live.

3

All those things happened when Veronica and me, we was both eight. I came to Highriver to live, Mrs. Bigelow got herself sewed up tight, and Sweet-Ho decided to give up her waitress life and settle down to take care of Gunther, who had just got born and dumbfounded everybody with his homeliness.

And *loud*. Sweet-Ho was accustomed to loud, working at Buddy Rivet's where they yelled in the orders to the cook through a cutout hole in the wall, like this: "VEAL SPECIAL, GO EASY ON THE GRAVY, AND A DARK BEER!" But even Sweet-Ho, she said she never heard *nothing* like that baby.

"I believe he regrets being born," she told me one afternoon when he was yelling away, with his face all purple.

"Was I like that when I was just born?" I asked her, after I peered into the drawer where we kept him, and observed him all scrunched with his little drumsticky legs pulled up and his mouth open.

24

"Shoot, no," Sweet-Ho said, looking at me surprised. "You was a quiet little thing. Sometimes I used to poke you awake just to make sure you was alive. Young as I was, I didn't know how else to tell except to poke till you jumped. And even then, mostly, you didn't cry. You just blinked your eyes like you was startled."

"*I* didn't regret being born, Gunther Bigelow," I told the baby, leaning over the drawer and shouting so that he could hear me above that screaming. "*I* was a quiet little thing." I poked him with one finger.

"Me too," announced Veronica Bigelow, who appeared at the top of the stairs. She never knocked, just came up the stairs and right in. Me and Sweet-Ho, we didn't care; we liked Veronica. "I was a quiet little thing, too."

She flopped herself down on a kitchen chair and fanned herself with a magazine that was lying on the table. It was hot. Already Gunther had heat rash across his scrawny shoulders even though Sweet-Ho sprinkled him three times every day with cornstarch. "My mama's home," Veronica said. "My father brought her home from the hospital, so I came to tell you to bring Gunther over to the house so Mama can see he's okay and begin to take care of him herself."

We all stared at the drawer where Gunther was. It was jiggling, he was screeching so hard. Sweet-Ho went over and looked in and made some kissing noises at him. "Shhhhhh, you sweet thing," Sweet-Ho said. "You're going home to your mama." And sure enough, Gunther shushed some at the sound of her

25

voice. He was getting to know her a little even though he'd only been around for two weeks. He liked Sweet-Ho. Everybody did.

But it was a mistake, sending him back home to his mama. Turned out that Gunther didn't like his mama much. Or maybe she didn't like him. She shook all over when she held him, and commenced to cry, Veronica said. So Gunther ended up back in his dresser drawer next to Sweet-Ho's bed and disrupted my sleeping habits for months on end, screeching as he did. But one night when Gunther was about seven months old I woke up like a shot in the middle of the night and saw through the dark that Sweet-Ho, she was sitting up too. But Gunther just lay there. He was too big for a drawer by then, and Mr. Bigelow had brought a crib down to the garage and wedged it in between Sweet-Ho and the wall. Gunther was laying silent in that crib with his backside sticking up in the air and his eyes were squinched closed tight.

"Well, shoot, Sweet-Ho," I whispered. "He's dead. We're really in for it now. What're we going to tell the Bigelows?"

But Sweet-Ho said, "Shhhh," and she got up on her knees so's she could lean over and peer into the crib, through the dark, at Gunther. "He's breathing," she whispered. "He's asleep, Rabble. It's three in the morning and he's asleep." She said it in a voice of awe, as if some miracle had appeared standing at the foot of her bed, maybe Jesus all aglow and with his hands bloody and a forgiving smile, you know?

And I didn't blame her none because I felt the same

way myself. Gunther Bigelow, asleep; that's the kind of thing that "Hallelujah!" should be cried out loud for. For seven months he'd been screeching off and on through the night so that Sweet-Ho and me, we took turns jiggling his crib. Some mornings at school I'd be half-asleep during spelling practice, and it was because Gunther had been so wakeful all night.

But after that spooky quiet night when I thought at first he must be dead, Gunther always slept. Sweet-Ho and me, we could even eat Fritos and talk to each other after we went to bed, and giggle and sometimes sing, and Gunther never woke.

He grew. He increased in homeliness and had every ailment known to man or boy or beast: diaper rash and impetigo and pinkeye and allergies to everything, so that when he drank milk he sneezed and when he ate vegetables he puked and when he ate Gerber Junior dinners his eyes got all swole up and itchy.

He could eat bananas okay, and hard-boiled eggs, and Chef Boyardee spaghetti. So he ate those three things, and grew. He hiccuped all the time, but we got used to that and even appreciated it after he started to walk, because it meant we could hear him coming.

When he was two years old, he moved back to his own house. His mama hadn't changed none, couldn't manage any better, but Gunther was old enough to fend for hisself at night, and during the day Sweet-Ho was there to hand him his bananas and such. Mrs. Bigelow didn't even seem to take no notice that he was living there. It wasn't like when I was little and

27

went to Gnomie's to live. Even though I don't remember it, Sweet-Ho said that everybody just fitted me in and made me part of the family. But it wasn't like they didn't notice. It was that their loving came so natural.

Me and Sweet-Ho and Veronica and her daddy all tried to be extra-loving to Gunther so's he wouldn't be aware that his mama's smile didn't mean nothing at all. By the time me and Veronica was twelve and doing the family trees, Gunther was four years old and was the sweetest little boy in Highriver even despite his homeliness and the fact that he had ringworm that September to boot.

Mrs. Hindler gave us a week to work on family trees. Me and Veronica, we got done real quick because we could work together in the evenings, and because I could loan her my cousins and all. We was all done by the weekend, but we didn't have to hand them in until Monday.

On Saturday, it was hot, like it always is in September. September's a funny time of year, because school starts but the weather still feels like summer. We was lounging around out in the yard, all bored and lazy. We had a stack of old *Reader's Digest*s that Mr. Bigelow had brung home from his real estate office. He said his customers was starting to complain that the reading material was old. And it was; some of them magazines dated back four or five years, but shoot, a *Reader's Digest* don't suffer much by age. Me and

Veronica, we was reading all the "Life in These United States" out loud, taking turns.

Gunther was with us. I looked over at him and smiled — he had purple medicine smeared on his ringworm, so he looked odd — and he grinned his sweet little grin back at me.

"Sometimes it seems like Gunther's my brother instead of yours," I told Veronica.

"Hey, Gunther, what's your full name?" Veronica called. He was just sitting there in the grass nearby, hiccuping and playing with a bug.

"Gunther Philip Bigelow," Gunther said, and hiccuped. He could talk real good for his age, and had been saying his whole name out full like that from the time he was only one year old.

"See, he's my brother," Veronica said. "If he were your brother, his name would be Gunther Starkey."

"Well, shoot, Veronica, I *know* that. I just meant it *seems* like he's a Starkey because he stayed at our place so long when he was little, and Sweet-Ho is motherly to him, and all."

"Sweet-Ho is a motherly sort of person," Veronica pointed out, even though I knew it already and she *knew* I knew it already. "And my mother doesn't seem to be, not anymore anyway."

She said it all matter-of-fact, but I knew what a sorrow it was to her. Veronica's mother was just about the biggest failure of a mother I ever knew, except for a black-and-brown spotted dog my Uncle Furlow had once when I was little. That dog had three puppies and squashed every one of them dead by laying down

29

right on top of them after they was born, and then pretended it was an accident. Me and Uncle Furlow knew better, though, 'cause we seen her do it, and we seen that she looked around real careful, arranging herself just right, then *squash.* So fast there wasn't nothing we could do, it took us by surprise even though we was watching.

I don't mean to say that Mrs. Bigelow would ever squash anybody, child or grown-up, or even want to, not even Gunther, whose looks was understandably a disappointment.

It was just that she didn't care about nothing, but pretended she did by that smile, which made it worse. Veronica told me that it wasn't always that way. When Veronica was little, her mama was normal-like, motherly same as Sweet-Ho for example, hugging and whispering and singing and patting, pouring cream and brown sugar over oatmeal, brushing Veronica's hair real careful so the snarls came out easy. Same as all mothers. And grandmothers too, I know for a fact, since I lived with my Gnomie all those years.

"It happened sort of gradually. The doctor calls it depression," is the way Veronica explained it to me. "Maybe it'll go away just as mysteriously as it began."

I didn't have much faith in it going away, though I didn't say so to Veronica. To tell the truth, to me it seemed as if it was getting worse, and Sweet-Ho agreed.

She looks okay, Mrs. Bigelow does, combs her hair and all and keeps herself neat. Lately she cries some, in her room, and maybe she smiles while she cries, we

don't know. She don't talk. And she don't do much —
Sweet-Ho cleans the house and cooks the meals —
but shoot, lots of people don't like to do much. My
grandma had a sister, my Great-aunt Patsy, used to
just sit in a chair and read the Bible all the time, moving her finger along the page and saying all the chap-
ters aloud in a mumble. But she was *normal*, just
Bible-oriented, and didn't much care for housework.

Mrs. Bigelow wouldn't be called normal. Depression, that don't seem the right word. Shoot,
everybody gets depression now and again, even me,
especially if it's raining out or if I didn't do my homework. I think *empty* is what you'd have to call her,
and isn't that the saddest thing, her with that smile
and all?

She does empty things. Things that don't hurt nobody but at the same time don't mean nothing. Things
like — well, here's one: Sweet-Ho told me that Mrs.
Bigelow goes around the house smoothing the beds all
the time. You know how a bedcover sometimes get
wrinkled up, or maybe it has a bump in it, like if
someone set something down and then took it away?
So you smoothe it over with your hand.

Mrs. Bigelow smoothes all the beds, again and
again, all day, even in the guest room, and no guest
has been in that house, ever, as long as I've been living
in the Bigelows' garage.

There was that one time after Gunther was born,
and they thought Mrs. Bigelow was acting normal.
But when she asked to have him back, and tried to
care for him herself, she smiled and smiled and shook

31

all over and then cried, Veronica said, when they put him in her arms.

"Don't you dare eat that bug, Gunther," Veronica said. Shoot, she knew he wouldn't. Gunther never ate nothing but bananas and hard-boiled eggs and Chef Boyardee spaghetti. He was just fooling with the beetle, making it walk on his arms and poking it with a twig to change directions.

Gunther messed with his little pet bug, and me and Veronica with the *Reader's Digests,* and it was hot, one of those real hot days with no air to it except thickness that you breathed in.

I think Mrs. Bigelow was laying on the glider on the back porch. Sweet-Ho was worried about her because she seemed worse. Maybe the hot weather was doing it. She smiled more and cried more, in her room, and walked around more, in the house, back and forth, back and forth. Sometimes, lately, she'd say things, religious-type things, usually, but they didn't make no sense to anybody. "He who believes in me shall not perish," she'd say to herself again and again. "Blessed be the pure in heart. The pure in heart." Then she would lay down, maybe pick up a book, but she wouldn't read; she'd flip the pages first slow, then faster and faster, and finally get up and walk again, as if she was always looking for something that she couldn't find.

Anyways, I think she must've been laying there on the porch beyond the kitchen. She was all dressed up

that day in one of them filmy dresses she liked —
Sweet-Ho says it's nothing to wash them, right in and
out of the washer and dryer in no time, they're all syn-
thetic — and maybe she would've had a book in her
hands. But she wouldn't be reading it, only staring at
the pages, talking about the pure in heart, as she
flipped through. I think she must've been doing that,
but I can't say for certain.

We got bored with the *Reader's Digest*s, and
Gunther got bored with his bug. But there wasn't
much else to do.

"Wanta go talk to Sweet-Ho?" Veronica asked.

"She's ironing. It makes the whole kitchen hot. I
don't think I could stand it in there. I might faint."

Veronica nodded. "Anyway, we're supposed to
watch Gunther, and Gunther's supposed to stay outside and let fresh air get to his ringworm."

Poor old Gunther. Nobody but Gunther ever had so
many ailments, one after another. Sweet-Ho said it
was nothing short of amazing that he had such a good
disposition, because most people who had pinkeye
and ringworm and impetigo all in the space of one
summer would get pretty grouchy, but not Gunther. I
guess he was just used to it. Gunther thought it was
normal to eat canned spaghetti for breakfast and then
have medicinal ointment smeared on him. Shoot, he
never knew anything else from the time he was a
baby.

"Let's go down to the creek, then. Maybe it'll be
cooler down by the creek. We can take Gunther wading, and we can look for frogs."

So we decided to do that, and I ran in to tell Sweet-Ho where we was going, while Veronica stacked up the *Reader's Digests* so's we could look at them later and maybe do the "Humor in Uniform" out loud.

Sweet-Ho was ironing, like I thought, but she gave me some cookies for me and Veronica, and a hard-boiled egg for Gunther. Both refrigerators, house and garage, had a special supply of Gunther's eggs, with "HB" penciled on the shells.

The porch was right off of the kitchen, and Mrs. Bigelow must have been on the porch, like I said. But I don't remember. I didn't look. Mrs. Bigelow wasn't the kind of person you seek out. But I think this: that if she was on the porch, laying on the glider smiling at a book, she must of heard me tell Sweet-Ho that we was going down to the creek with Gunther. She prob-ably heard that, and lay there smiling, and maybe after a long time it began to take shape in her head, so that she began to think behind that empty smile: the creek. They took Gunther to the creek.

That's the only thing I can figure out about what happened later, that she heard me talk to Sweet-Ho, and that it took a long time to take shape in her mind, what she heard.

Anyways, I put the cookies and Gunther's egg in my pocket and went back out to the yard. Veronica had tidied up the *Reader's Digests*, and Gunther had placed his pet bug in a safe spot and was standing there hiccuping, with a look of anticipation on his homely ointmented face. He always got this sweet look of anticipation when something was about to happen, and Veronica had told him we was going to take him to the creek to look for frogs.

He trotted along behind us like a puppy and we headed down the driveway. The creek isn't far from the Bigelows' house, but first we had to get past the Coxes', where Norman was usually lying in wait, up to no good.

Norman has a whole storehouse full of bad things that he yells at Veronica and me. Here's a couple I've collected in my mind over the years:

"Veronica-Bonica Pigelow and her rotten piggy-wiggy brother, nyah nyah!"

"Parable Starkey-naked, nyah nyah!"

That's the kind of stuff he yells, and sometimes he throws stuff, like chestnuts from the tree by his house in the fall, or if he can't think of anything else to throw, he has this endless supply of paper clips because of who his father is. He has this way of zinging paper clips and it really hurts.

Norman's father is the head minister of the Highriver Presbyterian Church, and he has this office in their house, with all these paper clips and erasers and stuff. I do covet all that office stuff, but I would never in the world let Norman know that.

"Hey, Starkey, what's it like to live in a garage instead of a house, huh?"

That's what he yelled that day, when we passed on our way to the creek with Gunther.

And this: "You sleep in a *car*, Starkey-Parkey?"

At least he wasn't throwing stuff. Shoot, I don't

35

much care what he yells, it only shows his terrible up-
bringing.

Veronica yelled back: "At least she doesn't sleep in
a garbage can like you!" but I poked her and made
her quit because yelling back only pulls us down to his
level, that's what I think.

Gunther, he just trotted along behind, not even listening to Norman Cox because he was thinking about
catching frogs, I expect.

When we got past Coxes' we had only Millie Bellows's house to pass, and she was sitting on the porch
like she always does in good weather. Millie Bellows is
the oldest person I know, so old I can't even put a
number to it in a guess. Maybe ninety would be as
close as I would try. Old and pink and evil-tempered,
like a big old grumpy-faced doll setting there in the
rocker on the porch, watching what goes by.

It is almost hard to believe what they say about
Millie Bellows, that she had three different husbands
along the way, all of them dead now. Looking at her
propped up there all pink and scowling in her rocker,
with a blanket over her legs on the hottest day so far
this September, who'd ever think that someone would
even want to marry Millie Bellows? Evil-tempered
old thing.

Veronica and me, we always called out greetings
politely to Millie Bellows, in hopes that good manners
would rub off on her, even in her advanced years.

"Hello, Mrs. Bellows," we called.

"I declare, isn't it hot?" I added, because a com-
ment about the weather is always a courteous thing,

according to this column on etiquette I read in the newspaper.

"Don't let that boy tread on my grass," Millie Bellows called down from her porch in that old-lady, evil-tempered voice.

We looked back at Gunther, and he wasn't even nowhere near Millie Bellows's grass. He was tippy-toeing right down the middle of the sidewalk, watching for ants as he went, and hiccuping now and then.

Her dumb-ass grass was all brown from the heat anyways, and if old Gunther Bigelow was to step on it, it wouldn't show a bit. But Veronica took him by the hand, just to show Millie Bellows that we was watching out for him.

We nodded politely to her to call her attention to what good manners is like, and then in a jiffy we was past her property and headed down through the vacant lot to the creek.

4

The best time for the creek is spring, with the water rushing over the rocks, and it's ice cold then, too, so that if you dip your feet in they turn downright numb. In spring, around the creek, bright green grass shoves up all ferny and thin, trembling-like if the wind blows, and sometimes pale yellow flowers peek out, bashful, all through it.

But this was September, and the creek was always low by then. Warm and sloggy and brown, with the grass thick and scruffy by the edges where the rocks are. Dragonflies was everywhere, dipping and flying around, all shiny and breakable-looking. The rocks was warm and mossy and smelled of decay, laying out that way in the heat where stuff — plants or even small animals and such — sometimes died. Once me and Veronica found a snake laying there, hot and dry and dead. And once a frog.

But there was always billions of live frogs, too, and we could hear them chugging and burping even before we got to the creek, when we was still pushing through the high grass in the vacant lot. Gunther was holding onto both our hands, Veronica's and mine. He was scared of the high grass because he disappeared in it, and I sure don't fault him none for that. I'm scared of disappearing, too.

We sat down on the flat rocks by the edge, took our shoes off, and tested the water with our bare feet. In spring, that's the time when we all yell and squeal from the surprise of the coldness. But now, at the end of summer, it was like poking your toe into the bathtub. The difference was, your toe came out muddy and slick from the creek.

"Here, Gunther, hold my hand tight," Veronica said, and she walked with him across the slippery bottom, round the rocks.

"Here, frogs, here, frogs," old Gunther called in his little voice. He was only four, remember, and even though he was smart for four, still he thought them frogs would come and jump into his hand if he called.

"Sit here, Gunther, and be real still," Veronica instructed him. She lifted him up and set him down on a big rock in the middle of the creek. "You be real quiet and try not to hiccup. Just *watch*, and maybe we can get some frogs to leap."

Good old Gunther, he always done whatever you told him, and always with a look of pleasure like it never occurred to him that someone might do him wrong. Of course he hadn't ever known nobody but me and Veronica and Sweet-Ho and his mama and daddy. His mama had done him a disappointment when he was two weeks old and she couldn't pick him up for shaking, but he didn't remember that. And every day since he was two weeks old, people was nice to him, giving him bananas to eat and putting medicine on his ailments and stuff like that. His mama had that problem with emptiness, but he wasn't around her much, and when he was around her he probably enjoyed that smile because he was too young to understand the strangeness of it.

So Gunther sat up real still on the rock, with his little feet skootched up under him, and looked down at the water, holding back his hiccups and waiting for frogs to jump.

Veronica waded over to the other side of the creek, and me, I stayed on my side, with Gunther skootched up on his rock in the middle. I commenced to turn over some small rocks, because sometimes that made the frogs leap out all burping and offended at being dislodged. Veronica was doing the same on her side.

All of a sudden Gunther yelped, like a puppy.

"Shhhhh!" Veronica shushed him so's he wouldn't scare off the frogs.

But he whimpered, the way a puppy does after a yelp. When I looked over, I seen his face was bleeding. Not severe or nothing, just a trickle of blood coming down across his cheek. He was still just setting there the way Veronica told him to, not moving or nothing, but he made little whimpering noises and held his hand up to the place where blood was running on his face.

Then he got hit again, and this time Veronica and

me both seen it. It was a pebble chunked out of a set of thick bushes downstream a ways; it came full speed out of them bushes and zinged old Gunther right on the back of his neck so's he started to cry, and I sure can't fault him none for that.

I seen who did it, too, because he was looking out of the bushes.

"It's Norman Cox!" I yelled at Veronica.

Veronica and me, we both hesitated. Gunther was setting there on his rock, bleeding and blubbering. We could go out there and get Gunther, but then Norman would have all of us for a target and he'd still be in that bush with a whole supply of them pebbles.

"Let's get him!" Veronica yelled, and she started charging down the creek, wading through that sloggy water as fast as she could. "Stay put, Gunther!"

Good old Gunther, he always obeyed, even when he was in danger of getting chunked again by a stone. He skootched down smaller on his rock, like a bullfrog hunkered over on a lily pad, and watched. Blood was still running across his face, but he wasn't crying no more. He was too interested in watching what happened.

I followed after Veronica, heading for the bushes where Norman was hiding. He zinged a stone but it didn't hit nobody, just shot past my shoulder and landed in the creek with a plunk.

Veronica slipped once just before she got to the bushes, and sprawled in the creek for a minute, so's she was muddy and wet up to the armpits when she got her footing and stood back up. Me, I was wet from

41

splashing along behind her. The two of us, dripping wet and steamy mad, crashed through into the bushes where Norman was. Ordinarily I wouldn't take on Norman Cox — he's in sixth grade same as me and Veronica, but he's a lot bigger, he wears shoes the size of a full-grown man — but seeing poor old Gunther, who never hurt nobody, whimpering like that. Well, that gave both of us the strength and the nerve to go charging into the bushes with our fists flying.

Norman, he was laughing at first, until we landed a couple of punches and he could tell how mad we was. Then he got all confused. I think he was actually reluctant to punch at girls. Zinging paper clips and stones at girls and babies, that was one thing. But punching with his fists was something else, and he got confused.

All of a sudden, Norman, he yelled, "Jeezus, lookit that!" and he stood right up out of the bushes and pointed down to where Gunther was huddled on the rock.

"You just wait till your daddy hears that you yelled 'Jeezus', Norman Cox," I told him, but I turned and looked where he pointed.

It still makes my heart near stop to tell of what we seen. I think back on it, and I can see it in my mind's eye still, with everything moving sort of slow motion the way they do it sometimes on television or in the movies. I see it like that, slow and rolling, all the colors bright and real, but no sound. There must have been sound. Gunther must have yelled. But when I think back on it, I don't hear no sound.

What I see is this: Veronica and Gunther's mother, moving slow through the water of the creek, with her skirt hiked up so's her legs was all exposed, and even her underthings as well. And her hair was down, hanging loose. I never even knew Mrs. Bigelow had that long, hanging-down hair. Whenever I seen her up till then, it was always tied up tight in a knot. But here she was, moving toward Gunther, who was staring at her, all frightened-like. I suppose he'd never seen that hanging-down hair before, neither.

Gunther's face was bloody, still, though I think it wasn't running down no more, just dried there sticky on his cheek. And when his mother reached him there — this is the part that makes my heart near to stopping when I think back on it — she picked him up and held him the way you would hold a tiny baby, the way she never held Gunther when he *was* a tiny baby. And she put her face down close to his and we could see that she was licking the blood from his cheek. We could see her tongue, and Gunther's scared look. And she did, she licked at the blood the way a mother cat or dog would do for its baby.

Then — I can see this part still, too, slow and no sound — right there, standing in the creek, she pulled open the buttons on the top of her dress. I wanted to turn my eyes away. I was shamed on behalf of Veronica and I wanted to look away, but I was scared, so scared for Gunther, there in the arms of this woman who looked like a wild stranger with her hair all falling around her shoulders, and with one breast right there exposed, and Gunther grabbed up in her arms.

43

She tried to make him nurse. He squirmed and tried to wrest hisself away, but she grabbed and twisted at his face, where she had licked the blood, and she tried to make him nurse.

Now I can hear the sound, thinking back. Now she took Gunther and — still with her dress tore open — she put him in the water. Put his head under and all. Veronica and I both started to run back, splashing and slipping through the creek. We tried to get back to pull Gunther out, to pull his head up so he could breathe. We wasn't that far away. And so we ran toward them, and we could hear what she was calling out again and again while she held him down there in the water.

"I baptize thee!" she was crying out. "I baptize thee! Who believes in me shall not perish!"

Dragonflies was still darting all around, as if September hadn't changed none. But we could see the splashing where Gunther was fighting her, trying to get loose, trying to breathe. And Veronica and me could have got there and pulled him out. But Sweet-Ho got there first. Sweet-Ho came tearing down that bank from the vacant lot faster than anything I ever seen. She didn't even take off her shoes, just tore into that creek fully clothed and grabbed Gunther up from where he was.

It had all happened so fast that Gunther was okay, coughing all choky-like but breathing and everything. He probably hadn't been under the water for more than half a minute. As soon as he got his breath back he started to screech like I never heard Gunther screech, not even when he was a baby. Sweet-Ho held him against her for comfort. Then she handed him to Veronica because their mother needed comfort, too.

Mrs. Bigelow was standing there in the creek with her skirt hiked up and her bosom all exposed, and she was smiling same as always. Smiling and smiling and smiling, with that empty look in her eyes. Sweet-Ho, talking real quiet and calm, buttoned up her dress all gentle-like and took her hand. She led her up the creek bank and through the field toward home. Veronica and I followed behind with Gunther. He had quieted his screeching and was just shuddering and sobbing into Veronica's shoulder.

It was like we was a family, walking. It was like Sweet-Ho was mother to us all, firm and loving and holding the hand of the most troublesome child. The rest of us stumbled along, wet and scared, through the high grass, and not one of us knowing what had happened or what it meant.

We passed Millie Bellows's house, and I could see her there on her porch, peering over the railing at us, all curious-like, nosy, and evil-tempered, but she held her tongue and didn't call nothing for a change. She watched is all.

Off in the distance I could see Norman Cox, too, as we passed his house. He was standing on the steps watching, and for once he didn't call out nothing either. He had a scared look, same as us. Pelting pebbles and calling names, that was nothing special. But now it was as if there was something new in all our lives, and it might bring real harm.

45

5

Old Gunther, he wasn't any the worse for wear after having such a mortifying experience, being pelted with stones and licked and drowned and baptized all in the space of five minutes. But I suppose when you're only four years old nothing surprises you much.

Mrs. Bigelow went off to the hospital again, the very same day that she baptized Gunther in the creek. Sweet-Ho took her home and fussed over her, humming comforting songs and such, smoothing her hair, taking off her wet clothes, and then when Mrs. Bigelow went to sleep, finally, still smiling like she always done, Sweet-Ho called Veronica's father at his office, where he usually went on Saturdays. She told him in a solemn voice to get hisself straight home because there was trouble.

So he came home, and together he and Sweet-Ho helped Mrs. Bigelow into one of them gauzy dresses she always liked, and then he took her to the car. Me and Veronica and Gunther stood on the porch and watched. We was still wearing our wet clothes, but the hot sun mostly dried them after a while, until we was all three somewhat mussed and mossy-smelling, and later Sweet-Ho would look at us and wrinkle her nose and tell us to change.

She didn't wave. We thought she might, from the car — Mrs. Bigelow, I mean — but she kept her head down and didn't look back, so we was all three waving at nothing. The car kicked up some dust and pebbles from the driveway and then it drove away. Sweet-Ho had been watching from the kitchen door, and after they was gone she opened it, and we heard that creaky sound it always made. She looked at us standing there.

"It wasn't your fault," she said, all gentle-like.

Gunther wasn't even paying no attention. He was examining the spring on the screen door to figure out what made it squeak. And me, I knew it wasn't my fault. But I could see that Veronica needed to hear that. It was Veronica who looked at Sweet-Ho with questions in her face.

"I'm sorry," Sweet-Ho said to Veronica. "I'm sorry I didn't realize sooner that she was gone. I was trying to watch her real careful, because I could see that something in her imagination was making her more agitated. But I took my eyes away, thinking she was resting —"

"I don't know what you mean by agitated. She's crazy, that's what," Veronica said, looking at the porch floor.

"Your mama's sick, is all," Sweet-Ho said. "It's a good thing for her to go to the hospital. Maybe they can make her well. We have to hope that, anyhow."

Veronica nodded her head. "She scared me," she said in a whisper to Sweet-Ho.

"Come on in, all of you," Sweet-Ho said. That's when she wrinkled her nose, smelling us when we filed past her through the door. "Change out of those ruined clothes so that you smell human, and then come down to the kitchen and I'll give you lemonade."

"She did, Sweet-Ho," Veronica said, all desperate-like. "She scared me something terrible."

"I know." Sweet-Ho put her hands on Veronica's shoulders. She had a way of doing that sometimes, which made you feel how strong she was, even though her hands wasn't especially big, any more than the rest of her was. Shoot, I don't think Sweet-Ho ever grew none after she married Ginger Starkey. But she had this strength in her that you could feel when you needed to feel it.

I took Gunther on upstairs to clean him up and change his clothes, and Veronica stood there for a while with Sweet-Ho, feeling that strength.

At suppertime Mr. Bigelow came home, just him in the car, and he said that Veronica's mother would stay at the hospital for a while until she was better. We was eating in the Bigelows' kitchen, me and Sweet-Ho and Veronica and Gunther, when he came in, and he sat down at the table with us. Sweet-Ho handed him a plate with some food on it. Mr. Bigelow thanked her

48

and once or twice he picked up a fork and poked at the food, but I noticed he didn't eat none. Sadness makes you lose your appetite, I expect.

Veronica asked her daddy if I could stay after supper so we could finish working on the family trees. I was surprised because I thought they was already done. We each had them tucked in our notebooks to take to school on Monday. But I didn't say nothing, and Mr. Bigelow said sure, as long as Sweet-Ho didn't mind.

Then he stopped to think. "You know," he said, "in view of what's happened, I think it might be a good idea if you and Rabble stayed in the guest room tonight, Sweet-Ho. Would you mind?"

"Nossir," Sweet-Ho said. "I could be right there in case Gunther is wakeful."

Mr. Bigelow nodded his head. "I'd appreciate it," he said.

Veronica went with me down to the garage so's I could get my night things and Sweet-Ho's. Walking across the yard I asked her, "Why did you say we had to finish the family trees? I thought they was all done."

"Yours is finished," Veronica said in an angry voice. "But I'm going to make a new one. I'm not going to have my mother on my new one at all."

Later, after I had my nightgown on, I went into Veronica's room, down the hall from the guest room

49

where me and Sweet-Ho was to stay. I have to confess that I like Veronica's room, even all frilled up like it is. The bed has one of them roofs on it, all ruffles, and the wallpaper is a whole mess of flowers, pink and white. It's like a movie star's room, if you don't look at the wall where Veronica has taped up dog pictures right on top of the wallpaper.

Veronica was sitting there cross-legged on her bed, in her blue pajamas. She had her crayons all laying about on the bedspread, and a pack of construction paper spread out. There was a blue sheet of construction paper on a book across her knees, and she was drawing in a whole new set of apples.

I picked the old one up off the floor where she had thrown it, and looked at the apple that said "Alice Mayhew Bigelow." Veronica didn't look at me. I felt kind of timid, even though Veronica was my closest bosom friend. She was drawing in them new apples with hard, firm lines, but she hadn't put new names in them yet.

I watched her put in her own name, and then Gunther's, same as before. She looked up, finally.

"I *almost* needed to put in 'dec' after Gunther's name," she said. "She *almost* killed Gunther."

"She was only baptizing him," I said. "That's the way they do it down at the Baptist church, Veronica, dipping their heads right in under the water. It's not meant to kill, only to save. My grandma was Baptist."

"Well, my mother's not. My mother's Episcopalian, and at the Episcopal church they only dribble a few drops, *nothing near* like what she did to Gunther. And don't try to tell me, Parable Starkey, that at the Baptist church they do it with their dress all ripped open indecent."

"Well, no. Baptists are always buttoned up tight."

"So, see? She's crazy as can be, and I don't want her apple on my tree." Veronica bit her lip and bent her head and went back to printing names in the apples. She put in her daddy's name: "Philip Bigelow." Then she started in on my cousins, the ones I had loaned her.

I wandered over to the open window and looked out. It was dark outside, and there was a breeze, so that tree branches were moving. Through the big oak tree I could see one lighted window — the kitchen one — over in Millie Bellows's house, and I supposed that she was in there, puttering about, doing her dishes, grumbling and complaining.

Closer by, there was lots of windows lighted up at the Coxes' house. Mrs. Cox, she wasn't so bad; maybe she was playing the piano or writing letters or something. Mr. Cox, probably he was reading his Bible, or putting lots of papers together with his billion paper clips. Norman, I couldn't even guess, but I was sure he was up to no good. In school, Norman was always drawing pictures with bombs and tanks and laser guns and such; sometimes, when we was all supposed to be doing silent reading, Mrs. Hindler would walk all casual-like to the back of the room where Norman's desk was. Then she'd swoop down, pick up the paper he'd been drawing on, and hold it up with a look like she was holding something extra-distasteful. And

51

she'd say, "Weaponry again, Mr. Cox?" before she crumpled it and threw it into the wastebasket.

Looking over at the lighted upstairs windows in their house, I figured maybe Norman was in his room building weaponry for real. If the oak tree wasn't in the way — and maybe when the leaves came off later in the fall, it wouldn't be — he could aim something like a bazooka right into Veronica's window from their house.

It sent a downright chill through my spine, thinking about getting blasted with a bazooka while standing there all innocent, in my nightgown.

Gunther cried out suddenly from his room, a sleepy sort of wail, and we heard Sweet-Ho go in to him.

"Gunther *never* cried at night," Veronica said in that new, angry voice. "Never since he was a baby, till now."

She stared at the paper in her lap and suddenly commenced to scribble hard in that one empty apple, the mother apple. She scribbled it all dark green, so hard that a hole came through in the paper.

Then Veronica started to cry, too. Not a sleepy wailing like Gunther, but a choking, muffled-up crying that made her shake all over and cover her face with her hands. After a minute both Mr. Bigelow and Sweet-Ho heard it and came in to offer comfort. I crept away, off to the guest room, and went to bed, because I didn't know what else to do.

In the morning, me and Veronica helped Sweet-Ho do

the breakfast dishes. Mr. Bigelow, in his bathrobe, sat at the kitchen table with his coffee and the newspaper, and he read to Gunther from the funnies. Gunther was still in his pj's, eating his banana real careful-like so's he wouldn't smear it on the paper.

"See?" Mr. Bigelow said, pointing to the pictures for Gunther's eyes to follow. "Here Snoopy's walking down the street, wearing his helmet, and look, Gunther, here in the next picture, he says, 'The Red Baron fearlessly maneuvers his craft.' "

Gunther grinned and reached up with his nonbanana hand to stroke his daddy's cheek. I watched. I never before saw Mr. Bigelow early in the morning, not shaved yet, and I liked how sweetly Gunther patted his daddy's whiskers.

There was a knock at the kitchen door, and Sweet-Ho wiped her hands dry and went to open it. There was Mrs. Cox, all dressed for church, with an aquamarine hat perched on her head. She was all color-coordinated as if she was an ad for Sears, with aquamarine shoes, too, and a pink suit with aquamarine trim, and a pink ruffled blouse. Her lipstick was the same shade of pink.

Me and Veronica and Sweet-Ho was all dressed — not fancy, but dressed — and I looked over at Mr. Bigelow in his bathrobe, to see if maybe he was embarrassed. But he just looked up at Mrs. Cox and smiled hello.

She came in and laid a basket on the table. "I hope I'm not disturbing you so early," she said. "Norman and I are on our way to church — he's out in the car.

But I wanted to drop this little casserole off for you, Philip. And to say I'm so sorry for your trouble."

"Sorry for your trouble" is what folks in Highriver always say when something has gone wrong. It covers just about everything; me and Veronica even said it to Norman when his dog got squashed by the J. C. Penney's truck. You can say it if somebody's septic tank overflows or if they get the flu real bad and miss a niece's wedding in Clarksburg, as happened to Miss Elizabeth Stevenson over on West Stanley Street last spring.

"Do you have time for coffee, Mrs. Cox?" Sweet-Ho asked. "There's still half a pot hot."

But she said no. "Thank you, dear. But Norman's being obstreperous, as usual. I have to get him down to Sunday school, and the choir's holding an extra rehearsal before this morning's service. So I mustn't be late. You'll let me know if I can be of help?"

When she was gone, me and Veronica lifted the foil on the top of the casserole to peer inside and see what it was before Sweet-Ho put it in the refrigerator.

"Chicken with stuff on it," Veronica announced.

Sweet-Ho leaned over and looked. "It's that *Family Circle* recipe she uses," she said. "She always brings this to PTA potlucks. It's pretty good, too. We can have it for dinner."

"Look!" Veronica said, and she pointed through the kitchen window. "Here comes Millie Bellows!"

We all looked, and it was true. Millie Bellows, wearing the same old housedress she always wore, hunched over and with her face scrunched into a frown almost as scary as a fist, was inching her way down the road toward the Bigelows' house. She was carrying a plate with a bright red shiny mound on it. The mound was wobbling with each slow step she took.

"Lord, she's bringing us a molded salad, and it'll melt in the sun before she ever gets here," Sweet-Ho said. "I'll go meet her."

She did, and when she came back with the dripping plate of Jell-O — it had marshmallows and grapes in it — she said, "She didn't want to come on in. Had to go home and watch her TV shows. But she says she's sorry for our trouble.

"Maybe this'll harden up some before dinner," she added, and put the salad in the refrigerator. "Don't you worry, Gunther," she said, seeing his face, "you don't have to eat it, or the casserole. I'm going to heat up some nice spaghetti for you."

Later, Veronica and me were sitting up in the oak tree at a place we had where the branches came together in a comfortable way.

"We should call this the Family Tree," I said. "You could fit a whole family right up here."

Veronica laughed. "Can't you just see my mother sitting up here, smiling and talking about the pure in heart?"

It made me feel better, that she was talking about it without that anger. But I didn't know just how to answer, so I just got all jokey. "We could set Millie Bellows up over there on that limb," I said, "and all the Coxes — they could perch over there, even Norman with his supply of paper clips."

Veronica grinned. "Norman could pelt people with paper clips, and Millie could grumble, and Mr. Cox could give a sermon, and Gunther could hiccup —"

"Mrs. Cox could sing that horrible solo she always does at weddings," I added.

"And my crazy mother could baptize everyone, and you and me, Rabble —"

"We could laugh," I suggested.

We did. We started in giggling.

"It sure wouldn't be an apple tree," Veronica said. "A *nut* tree, that's what it would be."

Secretly I was glad that Veronica was laughing again, same as before, because I surely didn't know what to do when she cried.

6

I find it powerfully amazing how things go on just the same even after some enormous change has taken place.

Places where they have great earthquakes, when skyscrapers and hotels fall down and holes open up in the ground and swallow cows and cars? People go on living there, and after a while they build other buildings and buy new cows and cars, and talk about gossip and weather and such. Just as if the thing never happened.

When Dorothy got back to Kansas after being in Oz? She probably just went back to school, same as always, and took spelling tests and played kickball at recess, I expect.

I bet anything she had nightmares now and then, though.

Me and Veronica, we went back to school on Monday morning, and she even handed in her original family tree with her mother's name. Nobody — not even Norman Cox — said nothing about what had happened, though they all knew. In Highriver, when there's trouble, everyone knows.

Mrs. Hindler hung all the family trees around the room, right out there for everyone to see. Nobody objected, but I thought it was real tasteless to do that, exposing everybody's family like that. Maybe there was stuff people didn't want anyone to know. I didn't go up close to examine them or nothing, but just from my desk I could see some stuff I hadn't known before — like Diane Briggs had one time had a sister who died. There it was, on her tree: Shirley Ann, Dec., age 1.

And over on the other wall — I couldn't see it real plain from my desk, and I surely didn't want to go up and peer intently at it — but it appeared that Parker Condon's grandmother had been married two times. Now wouldn't you think that should be kept private?

I like Mrs. Hindler a lot, but I believe she doesn't understand about privacy very well. All those secrets were there hanging around the sixth grade room exposed, and for all I could tell, she planned to let them hang there all year.

Corrine Foster's mother was expecting a baby around Thanksgiving. *That* surely wasn't a secret, what with all the baby showers people was giving for her already. Fifty people came to the one down at the Presbyterian church, and she got so many little jumpsuits that Sweet-Ho said she wouldn't even need to wash them, she could throw them away after each wearing, though of course it would be wasteful. I wondered if Corrine would climb on a chair with a crayon to add a new little-bitty apple to her tree when the baby came.

There hung Mrs. Bigelow, the mother apple on Veronica's tree. Of course no one sneaked over to climb up and pencil in "Crazy" after her name, but I wondered if the thought might be in people's heads.

There hung my tree, with the father apple crayoned in "Ginger Starkey" with his date of birth, and no one asked "Who's he?" (course they could see, he was my father) or worse: "*Where's* he?" I wondered if people thought it should be penciled in: Gone. Which is, of course, a form of dec.

It was time for English, and we all sat there at our desks, expecting that Mrs. Hindler would say, same as always, "Get out your *Understanding Grammar* books, people." But she didn't. Instead, she picked up a fat book off her own desk and held it up.

"Who here has heard of a thesaurus?" she asked.

Stupid old Roger Watkins shot up his hand fast as anything. I laughed inside myself. Roger Watkins never *listened;* he always just shot up his hand and gave wrong answers.

Mrs. Hindler looked around to see if anybody else wanted to answer. But Roger Watkins was the only one, and finally she called on him, though you could tell she didn't want to. He was waving and waving his grubby old hand in the air.

"Our bull is named that," he said. Everybody in the class burst out laughing, all but Mrs. Hindler.

"Your *what?*" she asked, with her face all puzzled.

"Our bull is named Taurus," Roger said. Everybody screamed with laughing. Dumb old Roger. That big old Taurus, he was the meanest thing. Once he bashed a dent in Roger's daddy's pickup; of course it was stupid as anything that Mr. Watkins drove the pickup right into the pasture where Taurus was laying in wait.

Mrs. Hindler nodded politely. "Quiet, people," she said. "Roger, you weren't listening carefully. Class, what did I say?"

Everybody called out different stuff. "Thossrus!" someone called, like a rhyme with rhinoceros. "Thorrus!" "Trocerus!" "Triceratops!" someone yelled, and we all laughed, because we remembered triceratops from third grade when we all studied dinosaurs.

She wrote it on the board in her neat printing. "Thesaurus." She pronounced it slowly and we all said it after her.

Then she explained how it worked. I was some startled that I never knew about a thesaurus before, because I've always been interested in words. I was only nine the year that I told Sweet-Ho the only thing I wanted for Christmas was a dictionary, and I wasn't showing off, either. She gave me a good one and I keep it right there on the table beside my bed, and consult it from time to time, or sometimes just read through it a bit for extra knowledge.

But I have to confess that a thesaurus beats a dictionary, and now I know for sure that I want one of my own, to keep. Mrs. Hindler passed them out to the class, but just old cheap paperback ones, and we would have to give them back after we got finished with learning about them.

Then, holding hers up with her pointy fingernails, she showed us how we could choose a word — almost any word — and look it up, and find all the other words we could use in its place.

"Who would like to choose a word?" she asked, and lots of hands shot up, including mine and Veronica's. Mrs. Hindler called on Corrine Foster.

"Love," Corrine said, and everybody laughed. Corrine blushed. She blushes real easy.

Mrs. Hindler told us all to turn to the index in the back and look up "love".

Right away I could see that it was an amazing thing, because I could see that there are all kinds of love.

Desire.

Courtesy.

Affection.

Those were just some.

"Let's look at 'affection', class," Mrs. Hindler said. And she showed us how to find the number, and turn there in the thesaurus.

Well, that was even more amazing. There was a *whole page*. You could hear everybody in the class murmuring out loud, reading all the words.

Not me. I read them to myself, feeling something like a shiver up my back at all the affection on that page.

Fondness. Tenderness. Regard. Admiration. Devotion. Infatuation. Rapture. And those were only a few.

Brotherly love. Maternal love. All different kinds.

I felt a real true fondness and devotion to Mrs. Hindler for showing me this.

We did a couple more words — though none was as exciting as love and affection — and then she gave us an assignment for homework. She handed back the compositions that we wrote last week. She had given us a choice for that assignment, and it had been a hard choice, at least for me. "My Ambition." Or "My Home."

Veronica had chosen "My Ambition" and had written her two pages about ballet dancing. She had confided to me that she wasn't real entirely sure that ballet dancing was her ambition, even though she went to Miss Charisse Balfour's classes every Thursday after school for four years, and had done a solo called "Sleeping Beauty Awakes" at the recital last spring. She didn't say so in her composition, but Veronica had told me that the toe shoes hurt and she didn't really think she wanted to spend her whole entire adult life with mashed-in toes.

Me, I have some ambitions, but they're all private ones, not things I want to tell the whole entire sixth grade. I was tempted to make one up, like "Female Spy" or maybe "Lady-in-waiting to the Queen of England." But I didn't want to appear foolish. So I wrote about "My Home," which was tough since my home was somewhat unusual, being a garage. But Sweet-Ho had explained to me, when I was biting on my pencil eraser and complaining about how hard the writing was, that "home" doesn't necessarily mean "place". It means feelings, Sweet-Ho said, about family. Realizing that made it easier for me to write those two pages.

Now Mrs. Hindler handed all the compositions back, but they didn't have any grades on them, not even the usual comments about neatness and spelling.

"I want you each to choose ten words that you've used in these compositions," Mrs. Hindler said, "and change them, using your thesaurus. See if you can make your writing more powerful, more colorful, more interesting."

Of course lots of kids, mostly boys, felt compelled to call out dumb stuff. Sometimes I wonder how Mrs. Hindler manages to keep her patience.

"Can we change 'and'?" yelled Norman Cox, the idiot.

Albert Washington raised his hand and asked, "What if nothing needs changing? What if it's just right the way we wrote it?" Everybody laughed, even Mrs. Hindler. Albert Washington is this black kid with glasses, and he always has the highest marks in the class. He's the youngest one in sixth grade, too, because he skipped second and fourth both. Albert Washington could read when he was three years old.

"You give it a try, Albert," Mrs. Hindler said. "If you can't make it better, then make it *different*, at least."

"Can we change the same word twice?" asked Parker Condon, kind of shy. He didn't mean it to be rude or silly. Parker Condon always got all nervous, trying to do things absolutely right. His father got powerfully upset if he didn't get all A's.

"I'm going to let you each use your own judgment," Mrs. Hindler said. "Maybe you'll find it a challenge to change the same word more than once, or maybe not."

Parker Condon started right in fidgeting. One thing I've observed is that people whose parents want them to get all A's all the time get nervous and fidgety if they have to use their own judgment about stuff. Because they worry that their own judgment might be a B instead of an A.

Other people asked questions, some rude and some not, but I quit listening. I read my own composition again, to myself.

MY HOME

My home has a lot of stuff in it that I like. It has: a dictionary which is mine alone; patchwork quilts made by my grandmother, who is dead, on the beds; a cookie jar shaped like a fat bear whose head comes off and that is the lid; a pillow filled with pine needles that make it smell good, bought at the church fair last winter; a toaster which makes your face look fat and odd if you look into the side of it; and a jar of pale blue glass which sits on the table and holds flowers all summer long.

My best friend can come there any time she wants, without even knocking, and she is always welcome.

At night, in my home, you can listen in the dark and hear stuff like doves, tree frogs, wind, or rain. That is all outside stuff. But there is inside stuff, too. Sometimes at night, after I am in bed, I can hear my mother, whose name is Sweet Hosanna, singing. She sings in a low voice, so as not to disturb me if I'm sleeping, and she sings hymns that she learned in her childhood, from her own mother.

All of those things combined give my home the good feelings that it has. Feelings are the most important thing in a home.

In the evening, after supper, in the Bigelows' kitchen, I read it again to myself and underlined in pencil the ten words I wanted to change. Veronica sat across from me and did hers at the same time.

Dead, I underlined. Smell. Good. Fat. Glass. Friend. Welcome. Dark. Disturb. Important.

Then I got out my thesaurus and began to work. My composition, when I finally finished, read like this:

MY HOME

My home has a lot of stuff in it that I like. It has: a dictionary which is mine alone; patchwork quilts made by my grandmother, who is dead (LIFELESS), on the beds; a cookie jar shaped like a fat bear whose head comes off and that is the lid; a pillow filled with pine needles that make it smell (GIVE OUT A SCENT) good (ATTRACTIVE), bought at the church fair last winter; a toaster which makes your face look fat (PLUMP) and odd if you look into the side of it; and a jar of pale blue glass (CRYSTAL) which sits on the table and holds flowers all summer long.

My best friend (COMRADE) can come there

any time she wants, without even knocking, and she is always welcome (RECEIVED WITH OPEN ARMS).

At night, in my home, you can listen in the dark (BLACKNESS) and hear stuff like doves, tree frogs, wind, or rain. That is all outside stuff. But there is inside stuff, too. Sometimes at night, after I am in bed, I can hear my mother, whose name is Sweet Hosanna, singing. She sings in a low voice, so as not to disturb (DIS-TRESS) me if I'm sleeping, and she sings hymns that she learned in her childhood, from her own mother.

All of those things combined give my home the good feelings that it has. Feelings are the most important (VITAL) thing in a home.

Then I had to copy the whole thing over, and fix up some awkward-sounding stuff, like "give out a scent attractive," which didn't sound right. I changed it to "give out an attractive scent." I figured Mrs. Hindler would see that I was using my own judgment, like she said we should.

Then I helped Veronica with some of her words, since she wasn't done yet. It took a long time, and finally, just as we were finished, Sweet-Ho said, "It's late. You two had better get upstairs to bed."

"Are we sleeping here still?" I asked her.

Sweet-Ho said yes. "Mr. Bigelow thinks we should stay over here while Veronica's mother is away. You don't mind, do you, Rabble?"

I shook my head. I didn't mind at all. I liked it there. But it made my composition seem like a lie. "If it's going to be for a while, can I move some stuff over from our place?" I asked her. "The blue glass jar, and my dictionary? Small stuff like that?"

"Sure. There are some things of mine I'll want to bring over, too. We can do it tomorrow."

So the composition was okay after all. The feelings would be just the same, and it was like I said: Feelings are the most important thing in a home. *Vital.*

7

One week went by after another, and I knew that summer had ended for sure when Sweet-Ho threw away the last of the chrysanthemums from the blue glass jar in our room, poured the water out, and put in a bouquet of dry red leaves from the big oak. The cool weather made Gunther's skin clear up some, so the scabs and rashes faded, and his cheeks turned rosy when he played outside.

Mr. Bigelow took Gunther downtown one Saturday afternoon for new sneakers, and he bought him a green corduroy jacket with a plaid flannel lining and a matching hat with earflaps. Wearing his new green outfit with the hat buckled under his chin, Gunther sat on his daddy's lap and helped steer the car all the way home. We could see him coming up the driveway, steering real careful with his daddy's hands atop of his, and his face all scrunched up serious.

When they got out of the car, Mr. Bigelow reached into the backseat and took out packages. He handed one to Veronica, one to me, and one to Sweet-Ho. "Surprises!" he said with a big smile on his face.

We opened them up, back in the house, and found he had bought us each a sweater: blue for Veronica, bright yellow for me, and a soft pink for Sweet-Ho. Veronica said "thank you" all nonchalant-like — she was used to her daddy bringing her things because he did it all the time — but I just stood there, rubbing my hand over the softness of mine, and even though I said it, because I was brought up proper, "thank you" didn't seem enough. I looked over at Sweet-Ho, holding hers in her arms, and could see she was feeling the same way.

Nobody had ever brought Sweet-Ho and me presents when it wasn't even Christmas. It was the first time.

That night, after supper, Veronica said, "We have to plan Halloween costumes. For Gunther, too. Gunther's big enough to go with us this year."

Gunther's face lit all up when we explained trick-or-treating to him. We had to gloss over the candy part, knowing Gunther wouldn't eat candy. "They'll give bananas to you, Gunther, I'm sure of it," Veronica told him. And to me she whispered, "You and me, we'll eat his candy."

"When I was a little boy, I was a ghost one Halloween," Mr. Bigelow said. "My mother just hung a sheet over me."

"You wanta be a ghost, Gunther?" I asked. But Gunther shook his head no. He was opinionated about such things.

"How about a clown?" Sweet-Ho suggested. "I believe I could turn his red sleeper suit into a clown costume, and we could make a pointed hat to go with it."

But Gunther shook his head no to a clown.

"Maybe, Gunther," I said, "you could wear your new green coat and hat, and we could make you into a dill pickle. We could make it all warty looking somehow."

But he said no.

"I know!" Veronica said. "We still have all my old dance recital costumes. How about a ballet dancer, Gunther?"

And Gunther began to grin. "With dancing shoes, too," he said. "And a magic wand with a star."

So Sweet-Ho scooted up to the attic where the old clothes were, and she came back with the bag of old costumes. We dressed up Gunther right there in the middle of the living room, first in pink tights — they bagged at the knees because they was too big, but Sweet-Ho said she could tighten them up a bit with a needle and thread — and then in the little blue net skirt with a billion layers so it stuck out all around and he looked like a flower.

"It's called a tutu," Veronica explained importantly.

"Too-too," Gunther said, and wiggled his behind.

Then he sat on his daddy's lap and Mr. Bigelow put the old pink toe shoes on him, and laced the satin ribbons up his legs over the tights.

Gunther fell at first when he tried walking, because

70

the shoes was too big — and toe shoes are hard to walk in anyway, I know because I've tried it — but then when he got the hang of it, he held his arms sticking out the way he thought a ballet dancer should, and he pranced around the room.

"I have to record this for posterity," Mr. Bigelow said, after he was able to stop laughing. He went and got his camera and took pictures.

The flashbulbs went off again and again as Gunther posed, dancing and stumbling, in the foolish tutu. Then, after we took the costume off him, Gunther posed again, all serious, in his new green outfit. Next Veronica and me put our new sweaters on for pictures. And finally, even though she got all embarrassed, Sweet-Ho agreed to put hers on, too, and he took one of the four of us together: Gunther on Sweet-Ho's lap, and Veronica and me arranged one on each side.

Mr. Bigelow said we looked like a bouquet of flowers.

That night before I went to bed, I put my yellow sweater, folded up, into the drawer where I keep my specialest things. In it I have a dried-up flower from Gnomie's grave; Sweet-Ho let me take it with me after the funeral back at the Collyer's Run Baptist Church. (I only got a B+ on my "My Home" composition after I handed it in. I would have got an A but it was dumb of me to say that my grandmother was lifeless. If I had used the thesaurus better, I would've chosen something else. There was lots of good stuff for "dead". "Depart this life", for one, or "Take one's last sleep". I'm certain I would've got an A if I had said my grandmother had taken her last sleep.)

Also in my drawer was my dictionary, and the thesaurus that Sweet-Ho got me down at Highriver Books and Cards when I begged. I have the blue ribbon I won for fifty-yard dash at the school track meet last spring. And two photographs of Sweet-Ho with Ginger Starkey, sitting with their heads close together, one with both of them smiling, the other with their tongues sticking out, looking foolish. There was four in the strip, which they posed for in a Woolworth's booth right after they got married, but Sweet-Ho cut it in half and gave me the bottom two. She kept the top. One of hers shows them kissing.

After I put my sweater in with all those other treasures, I put on my nightgown and got into bed. I looked around the room. Now it was filled with our stuff, Sweet-Ho's and mine, that we had brought over from the garage. Even the patchwork quilts that Gnomie made — they were on our beds instead of the plain white spreads that were the Bigelows' guest room spreads. My schoolbooks were piled in a chair. Sweet-Ho's old blue robe hung on a hook on the back of the door, and her hairbrush lay on the dresser.

She was still downstairs, and I could hear her and Mr. Bigelow laughing. She had gotten out the sewing box and was stitching up the pink tights so's they would fit Gunther's little legs, and I knew that they were laughing about that, about the thought of homely old Gunther being a ballerina.

In his little bedroom, Gunther was sound asleep,

probably dreaming about trick-or-treating in his tutu. And down the hall, I could hear Veronica still moving around in her room while she got ready for bed.

A night breeze was blowing, and I could hear the oak tree — the one Veronica and me called the Family Tree — with its last few leaves rustling, waiting to be blown off to the ground. The tip of one of its branches touched the window now and then. I turned off the light, and thought about all of that, and about the gift of the yellow sweater that was folded in my drawer.

It gave me such a strong feeling of belonging.

Trick-or-treating night was a school night, a Thursday. We was all ready. Mr. Bigelow had brought home stuff he got at the dime store: for Gunther, a pink mask of a lady's face, with bright red smiling lips, and a wig of golden curls. For me and Veronica, just plain old eye masks, which was what we wanted. We was gypsies, with bright scarves tied around our heads, shawls over our shoulders, and a lot of junk jewelry, some borrowed from Sweet-Ho and some from Mrs. Bigelow's jewelry box. She hadn't worn no jewelry for a long time, but she still had fake golden earrings, real gypsy-like, which Mr. Bigelow said we could wear.

"Is my magic wand ready?" Gunther asked, all anxious, after we had him dressed in his outfit.

It was. We had painted a cardboard star with gold paint and glued it to the top of a long stick from his Tinkertoy set with Elmer's glue. He took it from us and waved it about, dancing in his toe shoes. Sweet-Ho had stuffed them with cotton balls in the toes to make his feet fit in better. At first he couldn't see good through his mask, and kept bumping into things. But Mr. Bigelow got the idea to cut the mask eyeholes bigger.

So's he wouldn't get cold, we had painted his old blue flannel pajama top with marking pens, and now it was covered with red and yellow moons and stars, which suited his outfit just fine, and he could wear a sweater hidden underneath. It didn't even make him look too pudgy because old Gunther, he was so scrawny starting out.

Me and Veronica helped him down the back steps, because it was hard going in the toe shoes, and we started out, each of us carrying a big paper bag for treats. When we got down into the yard and stood there in the dark, Gunther shivered, looking around at our neighborhood in the nighttime and at three pumpkins with faces cut out and candles inside so's they glowed on our porch. But it was from excitement, not from being scared. He was already shivering from excitement back when we was still in the warm house.

We whispered to each other about should we go to the Coxes' house. If it was just me and Veronica, we wouldn't. We didn't mind Mr. and Mrs. Cox — they were really pretty nice — but somehow the thought of Norman rubbed off on the whole house and gave it a bad feeling, at least to us.

But Gunther loved Mrs. Cox especially. She knew

about his eating habits and didn't fault him none, and always at Easter she brought over special decorated eggs with his name painted on, knowing eggs was one of the things he ate.

"Norman'll be gone," Veronica said to me. "He always goes out all over town on Halloween, soaping windows and stuff. Remember last year he got caught letting the air out of Dr. Briggs's tires?"

"Yeah, I heard the door bang earlier," I said. "I'm sure he's gone already." But at the same time I said it, my eyes were darting around, checking the bushes and such, to make sure he wasn't lying in wait.

"Come *on*," said Gunther, all impatient, and he tugged at my gypsy skirt.

So we took his hands and headed across the yard, around the oak tree, to the Coxes'. On their porch we lifted Gunther up so's he could push the doorbell. It was one of them real chimey ones that played a sort of tune.

Mrs. Cox came, wearing an apron, and pretended like she didn't recognize Gunther. "It's a ballerina!" she exclaimed in a delighted voice. "Harold, come and see this *beautiful* ballerina with golden curls, right here on our porch!"

Mr. Cox, holding a newspaper, came into the hall and looked down over his glasses at old Gunther, who was hugging himself in excitement. It was the very first time that Gunther had ever been in disguise, except for when he was a baby and used to pull a blanket over his head and wait, giggling inside it, for us to find him.

"I declare," Mr. Cox said. "That surely is the most amazing ballerina I've ever seen! Do we have something to give him?"

"*Her*," Mrs. Cox corrected him. "It's a *lady* ballerina, Harold. Can you do a little dance for us, miss?"

Gunther held out his arms, waving his wand, and danced about on the porch. Then he bowed politely and the Coxes clapped their hands. Mrs. Cox put a banana into his bag, and she gave miniature Hershey bars to me and Veronica.

Gunther was truly gleeful after they closed the door. While we was helping him down the steps, he said again and again, "They thought I was a lady! They did! They didn't know it was me!"

We took him to some more neighborhood houses. People who didn't know Gunther so well, or his diet, gave him Tootsie Rolls and Charleston Chews, but he didn't mind; for him the fun was in the ballerina disguise — everybody admired it so — and the presents dropped into his bag.

It was beginning to get cold, and as we left the McCarthys' porch we could see Gunther shiver inside his outfit.

"We oughta take him home now," I said to Veronica. "Then you and me, we can do some more. We can go over to —"

But Gunther grabbed at my hand. "We didn't go to Millie Bellows's yet," he said.

"That mean old thing? We don't want to go there, Gunther."

But good old Gunther, he stood firm. "I *like* Millie Bellows," he said.

I looked at Veronica, and she shrugged her shoulders under her gypsy shawl. "Well," she said, "okay. Let's go there, and that'll be the last one, Gunther. After that one we'll take you home."

He shivered again, and did a little dance, partly to warm up, and partly because he hadn't tired yet of being a ballerina, and beautiful. We took his hands once more and headed toward Millie Bellows's house, a place I most surely didn't want to go.

8

Most nights are quiet where we live. Maybe you hear a dog bark someplace, or far off on the highway a screech of brakes now and then. And always at night, except in the hottest part of summer, you can hear the trees move in the wind. But it's a quiet wind.

But Halloween night was different. It was different because we were out in it, and most often after dark we were always inside, doing homework, watching TV, reading, getting ready for bed.

Out in it, in the dark, we could hear new sounds in the quiet night. Someone's cat ran across a yard, silent as anything, but the shrubbery rustled when the cat disappeared into the bushes, maybe chasing a chipmunk. Across the road we could hear the thud as somebody pulled a window closed. We could hear our own feet scuffle through the dry leaves that was all over the ground.

And sometimes we could hear the sound of running feet and muffled laughing. All the kids in town was out. Far down the road, under a porch light, we could see three people dressed as ghosts, with sheets over them, standing by a front door. Then, after the door closed, they ran down the steps and headed off in another direction, holding their sheet costumes up so they wouldn't trip over the dragging parts.

Everything seemed spooky and strange. A bush would move, and Veronica and me, we would jump, all startled, thinking someone might be hiding there. The wind blew the tree branches so that their shadows moved on the road in the moonlight, dark and scary, so different from the normal tree shadows in daytime.

Gunther tugged at us and we found ourselves nearing Millie Bellows's little house. Vines hung down from her porch roof. In summer they were shiny green, and we pretended they was poison ivy because we found Millie Bellows so poisonous herself; but of course it was only regular old vines, planted there for shade once and overgrown now because no one ever thought to trim them back. And probably years ago none of her husbands ever had the time, they was all so busy dying off one by one.

The vine leaves was all papery now, in October. Lots of them had fallen off, but the ones that still hung there was rustling against each other like the newspaper pages heaped on the couch Sunday mornings.

Millie Bellows, crabby old evil-tempered thing, hadn't turned her porch light on. Everybody left their porch lights on for Halloween, to guide the ghosts and gypsies. But not Millie Bellows. Not her. She probably hoped the kids would trip on their costumes, or on her rickety porch steps, and skin their knees. She probably hadn't even fixed any treats to give. She probably hoped no one would ring her bell.

But we lifted Gunther up so's he could, and when he mashed the button we could hear it buzz inside the house. There was a light on inside — we could see it through the curtains — and a TV playing. Even though he was chilly, Gunther was still prancing about, all cheerful, waiting to do another ballerina dance when the door opened. But the door didn't open, and we didn't hear no footsteps inside.

"She probably couldn't hear it, with the TV going," Veronica said, and she pushed the doorbell again, hard and long. "She's hard of hearing, being so old."

I didn't really believe that. Well, maybe she *was* hard of hearing, but what I thought was that she was just sitting all hunched up in front of the television, ignoring us. Shoot, the only time she ever paid attention to us was when she called scoldings from her porch — scoldings we didn't even need.

"She won't come," I muttered to Veronica while Gunther pranced, singing to himself, around the porch. "She hates us."

"Well, she did bring that Jell-O," Veronica said, calling my attention to the day that Mrs. Bigelow went away to the hospital.

"Hah. Melty old Jell-O," I said. "Here, let me ring it one more time." And I pushed the doorbell, holding it down with my thumb for a long, loud time. It was awful dark on the porch. Even with the moonlight outside, the creepy old vines made Millie Bellows's porch awful dark, and we could hear Gunther bumping into chairs as he twirled around in his ballet shoes.

"Shh! I think she's coming!" Veronica said. We all three stood still and listened. Sure enough, we could hear her shuffling toward the door. If I walked that way, Sweet-Ho would say, "Rabble, lift your feet, honey." But I suppose you can't fault someone so old for their walking habits. Maybe by the time you're ninety years old, you just keep grabbing onto the ground with your feet for fear you might be plucked up to heaven any minute when you're not dressed for it.

"Get ready to do your dance here in front of the door, Gunther," Veronica whispered. Gunther hitched up his droopy tights and got into his dancing position. Millie Bellows, muttering, pulled the door open so the light fell out onto the porch just like a spotlight falling over a dancer on a stage. Veronica and me, we hung back in the shadows, holding our bags and Gunther's.

"Trick or treat!" called out Gunther happily, and he danced about.

Suddenly out of the darkness in the yard something came shooting through the air. It missed Gunther, but it caught Millie Bellows, who was so hunched over she wasn't much taller than him, and she fell over on her knees, jarring the table in the hall behind her. We could hear glass break. Veronica ran forward to where Millie Bellows was crouched on the floor holding her head. But me, I turned and ran into the yard.

Once I got down the porch steps I could see a figure, even though he was dressed in black and running. I dropped the bag I was holding and ran after the figure — through Millie Bellows's yard and up the road, my feet pounding. Instead of my sneakers I was wearing these dumb black sandals of Sweet-Ho's because I thought they was gypsy-like, and I couldn't run as fast as usual because they was too big. But I set my mind to fastness and forgot everything else. I forgot the flapping sandals and I paid no attention when my shawl fell off my head and shoulders and dropped on the ground. I pulled my mask off my face so's I could see better and I kept my eyes firm on that black figure up ahead.

At the bend in the road he ducked into the woods. I was so close by then that I could still see the bushes moving where he had pushed through, and I went into the woods at the same place. But then I couldn't see nothing anymore — just thick trees and bushes. I stopped and stood still. For a minute I could hear someone breathing hard — I thought he was right there beside me — but then I realized it was my own breath. My heart was pounding, too, and I had a stabbing pain in my side from running so hard. But everything was quiet, and I knew I had lost him.

After a minute I turned and pushed back out to the road. There wasn't no point to chasing on through the woods. He could be anywheres.

I jogged back to Millie Bellows's house and on the way I picked up my mask, which was lying there in the road with its elastic busted. Farther down was my shawl, all dusty, and beside it something small and black. When I picked it up I could see it was a hat of some sort, and I rolled it up inside the shawl and carried them with me.

The door was still open and I could hear Veronica's voice inside. When I went in I had to step over a mess of broken glass, and I could tell from a handle on the floor that it had been a pitcher. Lying on the doorsill I could see the stone that the person in black — I knew it had to be Norman — had thrown.

I found Veronica in the front room, holding a dish-towel to Millie Bellows's face and patting at her as she lay on the couch. There wasn't any blood, just a swollen-up place by her eye.

"I called my daddy on the phone," Veronica said, "and he'll be right here."

Gunther was standing close by, with his ballerina mask pulled down so's it dangled around his neck. He was holding one of Millie Bellows's hands.

In the corner some newscaster on TV was talking, and then he showed a film of a building with its side blown out by a bomb. I went over and turned the television off. "He got away," I said. "I chased him but he got away."

In a chair beside the TV I spied a folded-up afghan all crocheted in shades of green and brown, a lot like one that Gnomie used to have. I took it over to the couch and spread it out over Millie Bellows's legs where they was sticking out from her flowered house-dress. Then I reached under and pulled her slippers off and tucked the afghan around her gnarly old feet.

It struck me that Millie Bellows wasn't talking none, wasn't sputtering evil-tempered comments like she surely had a right to. "Is she okay?" I asked Veronica.

Before she had a chance to answer, Mr. Bigelow came hurrying through the front door and over to the couch. He knelt down and examined Millie Bellows's face. Then he felt for her pulse, even though he's not no doctor or anything. He looked real careful at her little squinchy blue eyes.

"Millie," he said in a gentle, sort of joking voice, all reassuring, "I do believe you must have nine lives, like a cat." He put his arm under her shoulders and helped her to sit up.

She squinted around. "Where are my glasses?" she asked.

Gunther reached over to the table and handed them to her. "They're kinda busted," he said, sadly.

The glass wasn't broken, but the gold frame was all bent on one side. She tried to put them on, but you could tell it hurt when she touched her face, and finally she just held the glasses in her lap.

"Well," she said crossly, "how do you expect me to *see* anything?"

Mr. Bigelow took the glasses and pried at the bent part until he straightened it some. Then, real careful, trying not to touch the swollen-up place, he put them onto her. She blinked and looked around the room. "What was it broke?" she asked loudly. "I heard something break."

I ran to the hall by the front door and picked up the handle that was lying there in the pieces of broken glass. I took it back to her. "It's sharp at the end," I said, trying to be helpful. "Be careful."

Sitting up, Millie Bellows had been trying to get herself in order and to look dignified, but when she took that handle from me, and peered at it through her bent glasses, her face just sort of fell apart. She started to cry. "My mother's wedding-gift pitcher," she said. "It sat there upon that hall table all my life!" She turned the handle over and over in her hands.

"Me and Veronica'll try to mend it for you," I told her. "We'll use Elmer's glue." I knew we couldn't, but I thought it might make her stop crying if I said that.

Mr. Bigelow hugged her tight around the shoulders. "Millie," he said, "I have the car outside. And I'm going to run you over to the hospital so they can take an X ray. You look just fine to me, but we want to be sure."

She looked all confused, but she gave the handle back to me and swung her legs down to the floor. "Here," I said. "I have your slippers here." I knelt down to put them back on her feet.

But she kicked at me like a little child having a tantrum. "Shoes!" she ordered, frowning. "Get me my shoes."

Veronica found her Sunday shoes in the bedroom closet, and when Millie had them on, she stood up, leaning on Mr. Bigelow's arm.

"You girls take Gunther home, and tell Sweet-Ho not to worry," Mr. Bigelow told us.

So we did that, collecting our dumb old trick-or-treat bags from the porch as we went. Gunther

85

yawned and shivered all the way home, and we didn't talk much. Halloween was ruined.

Back home, while Sweet-Ho was putting Gunther to bed, me and Veronica examined the black hat that I had wadded up inside my shawl. It was just like a little beanie, and inside on the lining was printed: SENIOR CHOIR. FIRST PRESBYTERIAN CHURCH.

That didn't surprise us none.

9

Millie Bellows had to stay in the hospital overnight — for observation, they said. It made Veronica and me laugh, thinking of Millie Bellows being observed. Shoot, she was always the one that did the observing of everything, from her porch chair. I wondered if she was an old crosspatch at the hospital, complaining about the nurses and the food and who-knows-what-all.

Mr. Bigelow picked her up in his car and took her back home the next morning. After school, Sweet-Ho asked us to take over a casserole and some brownies.

"We ought to take the Elmer's glue, too," Veronica said, "and try to glue her broken pitcher."

So I put the little white bottle of glue in my pocket and we kicked through the leaves over to Millie Bellows's house, me with a shoe box full of Sweet-Ho's brownies and Veronica carrying the Bigelows' big blue casserole dish filled with beef stew.

Millie Bellows knew we was coming because

Sweet-Ho had called her on the phone, so we just knocked loud and went in. She was lying on the couch again, but with her glasses on; she was watching TV. Dumb old *Wheel of Fortune*, with Vanna White wearing indecent clothes and giving away diamond earrings and such to people who always say hello to their children back in Indiana.

"We're sorry for your trouble, Mrs. Bellows," Veronica said. "I'll just put this stew into your oven, and then it'll be hot at dinnertime. Would you like a brownie? And I could make you a cup of tea."

Millie Bellows gave a little snort, which Veronica took as yes. I sat down on a chair near the couch while Veronica went to the kitchen.

"Are you feeling better?" I asked politely. I could see that her eye was black. Actually, it was more purple than black.

"Shhh," Millie Bellows said, watching the TV. Somebody had just hit a BANKRUPT and was trying to look like a good sport about it.

Well, if a person don't want to converse politely, you can't force them. So I just watched with her while a man wearing a nametag that said DON bought some vowels and then guessed the phrase: "It never rains but it pours." He got to choose three thousand dollars worth of stuff from the game room, so he took a pool table and some water skis, and Vanna White pretended to be all delighted.

"It never rains but it pours" made me think of the busted pitcher, and I peered around to see if I could spot the pieces of glass. Mr. Bigelow had told us that he cleaned it all up after he got back from taking Millie to the hospital. I couldn't see it anyplace, and I sort of hoped he had thrown it away, because I knew that the Elmer's glue wouldn't work.

Finally Veronica came in with a tray full of tea things. *Wheel of Fortune* was just ending; Don didn't win the Volkswagen Cabriolet because he chose the wrong letters, so Vanna looked despondent, pouting, while the audience clapped, and then a commercial started.

"Did you bring sugar? I need sugar," Millie Bellows said. I got up and turned the TV off.

Veronica stirred some sugar into a cup of tea and handed it to Millie, who grunted and eased herself up into a sitting position on the couch.

We all sipped at tea without saying nothing, and then suddenly Millie Bellows burst out, "Why was your brother dressed in that ridiculous fashion?"

Veronica started to laugh. "That was his Halloween costume, Mrs. Bellows. He was supposed to be a ballerina. It was my old costume from a dance recital. We were trick-or-treating. That's why we rang your bell last night."

"Well, all that foolishness got me this eye, I hope you know that, and my head pained so I couldn't sleep all night. Lord knows what my hospital bill will be."

Mr. Bigelow had already told us that her hospital bill would be *nothing* because of her insurance and Medicare. But we didn't say nothing. She just needed to fume and fuss, I guess, so I can't fault her none.

"If you hadn't pushed at my doorbell in that *demanding* way, I would never have opened my door in that terrible wind," Millie Bellows muttered.

Terrible wind? There wasn't no more than a regular evening breeze the night before. But I kept silent, and so did Veronica.

"You ought never to open your door in a terrible wind," Millie went on, "for the very reason that something might blow in and do damage, as it did. Time you learned that."

We nodded and sipped at our tea. So she thought that the wind had blown something in and given her a black eye. Some wind that would be, to pick up a stone and hurl it. Some wind, wearing a black choir robe and hat from the Presbyterian church. But I didn't say nothing.

Millie Bellows stuffed half a brownie into her mouth and then just kept talking angrily, crumbs flying. "This *eye* will heal," she said. "But my mother's wedding-gift pitcher, now that is an absolute loss. My mother was married in 1890, and that pitcher was a gift from Mr. and Mrs. Leland Norton. Mr. Norton once owned the Highriver Coal Company, but of course you wouldn't care about that."

"Mrs. Bellows," I said, "we brought the Elmer's glue along with us, so's we could try to mend your pitcher." I took the glue out of my pocket and showed her.

"I know it's in a lot of pieces," Veronica told her, "but Rabble and I can work at it, and maybe —"

Millie Bellows squinted over at me. "Just what kind of name is that, anyway?"

"Elmer's," I said. "It's just a name for glue."

"*Your* name is what I mean."

"My name? Rabble? Well, that's short for Parable, Mrs. Bellows. It's a Bible name."

She grabbed up another brownie. "A Bible name is *Ruth*," she said. "Or Rebecca. Now those are good Bible names. I don't know what your mother was thinking of, to give you a name like that."

Of course it wasn't my mother at all who gave me my name. It was Gnomie. But I didn't see that it was any of Millie Bellows's beeswax. And shoot, I can't see as how *Millie* is such a wonderful name. Or that it was good manners to be shoving brownies into your mouth that way, and talking while they was still there, not even chewed. I thought all of that, but I didn't say nothing.

"Mr. and Mrs. Leland Norton lived in that big yellow house up on High Street," she was saying. "The one that's a funeral parlor now. In the old days it was the most elegant house in Highriver. When my mother was married in 1890, the reception was held at the Riverfront Hotel, which no longer exists, and the guest list numbered in the hundreds. They served chicken à la king in patty shells. Somewhere here I have the news clipping from the wedding."

She began to peer around the room. There was stuff everywhere: books and magazines and old photograph albums, all of it somewhat haphazard on top of unmatched tables and chairs. Old lamps was every-place, and vases, and framed photographs of people from the old days: ladies with their hair all swept up, and men looking stern, with pointed mustaches.

"I believe I won't look for it today," she announced suddenly, and lay back down. "See that you wash up these cups."

Veronica picked up the tray. "And shall we try to glue the pitcher for you?" she asked.

Millie Bellows waved her hand in the air and shook her head. Her eyes was closed. "It's ruined," she said. "Just clean up and then go home."

So we did.

When Sweet-Ho came to bed that night I was still awake, reading. I watched while she put her night-gown on and began to brush her hair.

"You're so pretty, Sweet-Ho," I said to her. "I believe you're as pretty as a movie star."

It was true. Her hair was long and thick, and it curled at the ends. She was wearing a blue flannel nightgown that matched her eyes, and it had a high neck with lace around the edge, so that she looked old-fashioned like the ladies in Millie Bellows's photographs, but softer and sweeter, not nervous and serious like the photograph people.

Our room at the Bigelows' house was pretty, too. It had pale yellow wallpaper the color of a winter sunset, with tiny pink flowers scattered about. We hadn't put up any of our old wall stuff from the garage, because Sweet-Ho said that thumbtacks or tape would mess the walls. But there was a little picture hanging between the beds, a watercolor of a garden, and it made me think of Gnomie's garden back at Collyer's Run, full of pink roses and tall blue delphiniums. Back before Gnomie got sick, she used to tend her flowers every day in summer, talking to them, telling them to stand up straight and proud.

"Millie Bellows really liked your brownies," I said, "but her manners is atrocious. She gobbled, and talked with her mouth full."

"She's old, that's all."

"Old doesn't excuse rude."

Sweet-Ho got into her bed and sat with her knees up and her chin resting in her hands. "She's lonely, too, I expect. If you live alone, you forget about the need to make other people feel comfortable. And that's all that good manners is: making other people feel comfortable."

I never thought about that before. But Sweet-Ho was right, I decided. Please and thank you and excuse me and not talking with your mouth full and all that, it's for the other person. And Millie Bellows, she didn't care none about me and Veronica.

"I'm going to try to remember that all my life," I told Sweet-Ho, "even if I get to be a hundred. But I don't expect I'll ever be alone, because I plan to have a lot of children."

"Good. I'll be a grandma."

"Sure. You can live with us and bake cookies and help tend the babies."

Sweet-Ho chuckled sleepily. She lay down and hugged her pillow. "You won't make me do the ironing, will you?"

I thought that over while I marked my place in my book and put it on the table beside the bed. "No," I decided, and turned the light out. "You won't have to do anything you don't want. You can be *lazy*, if you like."

"Indolent," Sweet-Ho said, yawning. "I'll be indolent when I'm old."

Shoot, Sweet-Ho always had me beat in words. Even now, with my thesaurus.

10

Fall continued on and began to turn into the beginning of winter, the way it does. Halloween pumpkins that had been standing on people's steps and porches turned rotten and their faces caved in like the faces of old people, squinched and wrinkled. Sometimes in the mornings, walking to school, Veronica and me could blow steam out of our mouths, and we pretended to be horses, snorting and prancing about.

We fell into the habit, afternoons after school, of stopping by Millie Bellows's house. We didn't do it because we *wanted* to. We did it for Sweet-Ho and for Mr. Bigelow, who asked us to, and only after we argued a bit.

"She's too old to be all alone all the time," Sweet-Ho had said. "She just needs someone to check and see she's okay."

"You could call her on the phone," I pointed out.

"Of course I could call her on the phone. But I'd

feel better if someone looked in and *saw* her regular. And I can't always do that, with Gunther to tend and all."

"Just a hello would be enough," Mr. Bigelow said.

"A *cheerful* hello," Sweet-Ho added, glaring at me.

Veronica and me made faces at each other. But we did it, each day on our way home from school. At first we just looked in and said hello — a cheerful hello. But before long we was actually going inside, making her some tea, helping her a bit about the house. Millie Bellows grumbled and fretted, complaining that we was always hanging about and in the way. Shoot, I couldn't fault her none for that; nobody wants people always poking their noses in your business. But there was always something that needed doing: one day a light bulb to be changed in a place she couldn't reach without standing on a chair — and she wasn't too steady on her feet, so it would have been downright risky for her; another afternoon, her kitchen sink all clogged up so that we fixed it with the plunger, some-thing she wasn't strong enough to do. Most days it was just her few dishes in the sink, or some little bits of laundry. We noticed that if we didn't do those things, she ate off the same dishes again without washing them, and wore the same clothes too long without changing.

She never thanked us, not once. She only sat in the front room watching her dumb old TV shows, and if we got to laughing in the kitchen she called out that we was too noisy. But after we finished the chores and made tea, she would turn off the set, get out her old photograph albums, and show us the pictures while we sat with her.

At first we only looked to be polite. But after a while, after she showed us the same pictures again and again, it got so's we felt we knew all those people with their high, stiff collars in the faded photographs. We got to wheedling her into telling us stories to go with the names.

"What was your brother Howard like when we was little?" Veronica asked. We was passing around Howard, in a picture where he was little and wearing an old-fashioned sailor suit with long white stockings, his hair down to his shoulders like a girl.

"Remember when we dressed up Gunther like a ballerina, he tried to act all graceful and pretty? When your mama dressed Howard up with long curls and stockings, did he act that way?" I asked.

"Good heavens, no," Millie Bellows said, and took the photograph back to peer at Howard. "He was all cleaned up to have this picture taken. But most times he was just as dirty and noisy and dreadful as that Cox boy."

Veronica and me didn't look at each other, but I know we was both thinking the same thing when Millie Bellows mentioned Norman Cox. Back at the house, we still had the black choir cap hidden in a drawer under Veronica's summer clothes. We hadn't decided what to do with it. We hadn't even told Sweet-Ho or Mr. Bigelow about it, not even after Halloween when they was still wondering and speculating about who could've thrown the stone.

"Tell us something dreadful that Howard did," I said. In the picture he looked so clean and sweet, about Gunther's age and ten times handsomer.

"Here he is, older," Millie Bellows said, and handed us another photograph of the same boy, with his hair cut short and parted in the middle. He was wearing a necktie and staring right at the camera all handsome and serious, and he looked just about our age, me and Veronica's. "Once he put half a dozen frogs into my bureau drawer, right in with my underthings. It startled me so that I came right close to fainting. Father whipped him for that."

Veronica and me both giggled. I stared hard at the photograph, trying to see mischief in the boy's eyes. But it was just a solemn stare back at me. There wasn't a hint of frogs or faints or whippings. Shoot, it's a downright shame how a photograph don't catch nothing but a single instant.

"Did he go to college? Did he get married?" Veronica asked.

Millie Bellows snatched the two photographs of Howard back, tucked them into the album, and closed it tight. "He would have," she said. "I'm quite sure. But he died when he was fourteen."

"How?" I asked, forgetting that it might be rude.

"Howard was always a disobedient, willful boy. Father was very strict about not skating on the river before the ice was frozen solid. But Howard disobeyed, Howard and a boy named Willie Morrison who lived

98

down the road. They both fell through the ice and were drowned." Millie Bellows glared at us as if maybe we caused it, and I could see she was still angry at Howard for dying on her and never putting frogs in her underthings again. Her face turned pinched and pained, remembering.

"I certainly hope you're not planning to run off without tidying these tea things up," she said with her mouth all pinched up. She always said that. It was her way of telling us to leave.

Walking through Millie Bellows's yard after we left, Veronica suddenly said, "Her grass is going to be ruined if nobody rakes these leaves up before winter."

"Well, shoot, *I'm* not going to do it. We're *already* doing her housework for no pay. Anyway, she has crummy grass. Her yard is the worst-looking on the whole road, because she don't take care of it."

"Doesn't."

I made a face. "Okay, *doesn't*," I said. Veronica is the only person in the whole world who I don't mind if she corrects my grammar. Mrs. Hindler corrects me, but I resent it some because she does it in public, in front of the whole sixth grade, though she don't — doesn't — mean to embarrass me, she just wants me to talk elegant.

"I got an idea, Rabble," Veronica said.

"What?"

"We still have that choir hat, and we never did anything to punish Norman."

"I told you we ought to take it to the police station and turn it in as evidence."

"The police wouldn't do anything. It's only circumstantial evidence anyway. Maybe the most they would do is call Norman in and talk to him, and they've *already* done that —"

"About a million times," I agreed. It was true. Norman Cox was always being hauled in for a talking-to by the chief of police. "What's your idea?"

"Blackmail him into helping Millie Bellows in her yard and stuff. It would be the best kind of punishment, Rabble, because it makes amends to the person he wronged."

"Raking a dinky old yard isn't much punishment, though."

"But there's other stuff. Her whole house needs painting."

We looked back toward Millie Bellows's little house. Once it had been white. But the white was gray now, and dirty, and the paint had bubbled and peeled and flaked. The vines that hung all about the porch had died in the cold weather, so's only the stems was there, twisting about, brown and stiff. Underneath all the tangle of vines and the wrecked paint, it was a pretty little house, with a nice shape.

"I would admire it yellow, I think," I said. "Not ugly old Day-Glo yellow like some of the houses over in that new development. But a deep, important kind of yellow. Like Gulden's mustard maybe."

"Gold," Veronica said. "That would be called gold."

"Shoot, Veronica, wouldn't that be something? For Millie Bellows to have a golden house? Maybe it

100

would cheer her up so's she wouldn't be such a grouchy old thing." I squinted my eyes, looking at the house, picturing it all fixed up. "We'd never get Norman Cox to do it, though. Never in a million years."

Veronica didn't say anything, and we started walking on toward home. "I could," she said, finally.

"Could what?"

"I could get him to do it."

I busted out laughing. "How?" I asked.

Veronica looked all shy. "Promise you won't get mad?" she said.

Mad at Veronica? Never in my entire life in Highriver have I ever once got mad at Veronica. She's my best friend. Like a sister. I was some startled when she said that. I just looked at her, puzzled-like, and she bent her head down so's I couldn't see her face.

"Norman likes me," she said.

I just stared. But as I stood there, staring at her, I knew it was true. While I wasn't even paying no attention, over the past weeks, Veronica had gotten taller and more filled out. Her hair was curly, not unusual-colored like mine, but even so, thick and nice. Her eyes was deep blue, and she had the sweetest smile I ever saw, bar none.

And I remembered the way Norman acted around her in school. Yelling insults, acting stupid and show-offy all the time. Sometimes he passed her notes in class, and they was always just dumb jokes or stupid drawings of warfare and stuff. She showed them to me before she crumpled them up. One recent one was a ballpoint-pen drawing of a fat hog wearing a sunbonnet, and a balloon coming out of its mouth said, "Oink oink." Underneath Norman had written "Veronica Pigelow."

When she showed me that one, she giggled, and I muttered something about how insulting it was. But now I remembered that the pig had a sweet smile. As pigs go, it was a pretty one. Remembering it, I knew what she said was true. Norman liked her.

"You're mad, aren't you?" Veronica asked.

"No. I was just thinking he has a dumb way of showing it, is all."

"Boys don't know how to act around girls," Veronica said. "So they do dumb stuff, like Norman, throwing stones and yelling insults. It's just a way of getting attention, I think."

"Maybe."

"I'll tell you something else."

"What?"

"Parker Condon likes you. He gets all nervous around you."

"Around me? Parker Condon's nervous around *everybody*."

Veronica laughed. "That's true. But especially around you, Rabble. I've been noticing."

I felt funny. I felt funny because I hadn't known.

"Here comes your daddy," Sweet-Ho said that evening to Gunther while he played on the kitchen floor. She was looking through the window. Gunther jumped up and ran to her to be lifted so's he could see, the way he did every night when Mr. Bigelow came home from work.

"Daddy! Daddy!" Gunther said, all happy, when Mr. Bigelow came through the door.

Sweet-Ho handed him to his daddy. "Hi, Phil," she said, and smiled when Mr. Bigelow hoisted Gunther up to his shoulders for a ride.

"Rabble and Veronica? Is the table set?" she asked. "It's almost time for supper. Put your cards away now."

Me and Veronica had been playing Go Fish at the kitchen table. We hadn't talked any more about Norman Cox. It was a thing we had to think about before we did more talking.

"You got any kings?" I asked. But Veronica had already commenced to gather up the cards, so I gave her my hand. She was winning, anyway. We started collecting the plates and silverware to take them to the dining room.

"Can I do the napkins?" Gunther asked, and his daddy lifted him back down so's he could help us. He was real good at folding the napkins into triangles and putting one beside each plate.

"I got a call at the office today," Mr. Bigelow said to Sweet-Ho. "From Meadowhill."

Gunther went on about his business, folding napkins real careful. Sweet-Ho kept right on stirring something on the stove, but she looked over at him with a question in her eyes. I counted forks and didn't say nothing. Veronica picked up a stack of five dinner plates and headed for the dining room, but I noticed she kept the door open so's she could listen from where she was.

Meadowhill was the name of the hospital where Mrs. Bigelow was. Where she had been now for two months. The doctors there had told Mr. Bigelow no visitors, not even family, at least for a while. He talked to them once every week; I knew because Sweet-Ho told me. They always said no change.

Veronica never said nothing about her mother, never asked nothing.

"Veronica?" Mr. Bigelow called. "Honey? Come in here for a minute."

Veronica set the plates on the table and came back to the kitchen real slow, with her eyes on the floor, like she might see something scary if she looked up.

Her daddy put his arm around her.

"I talked to one of the doctors at Meadowhill," he said. "And he said they'd like you and me to come for a visit on Saturday."

"Rabble and I have to help Millie Bellows on Saturday," Veronica said, real quiet. "We're going to scrub her kitchen floor."

"And wax it, too," I added. "We can take a can of floor wax from here, can't we, Sweet-Ho?"

"Self-polishing is what we need," Veronica said, still with her head down. "She has loads of rags there, old clothes all ripped up, so we don't need rags, but she doesn't have any self-polishing wax, so —"

104

Gunther trotted off happily to the dining room with his hands full of folded napkins.

"I'm very proud of you girls, for the way you've been helping Millie Bellows," Mr. Bigelow said, with his arm still around Veronica. "So is Sweet-Ho."

"I surely am," Sweet-Ho said, and she took the stew from the stove and turned the burner off.

"We won't leave till after lunch on Saturday, so you can do her floor in the morning if you want. And we'll be back by suppertime." Mr. Bigelow was looking at Veronica as he talked.

She finally lifted her head up. "Do I have to?" she asked.

He didn't say nothing for a moment. Then he said, "No. But I hope you will."

Veronica pulled away from him and picked up the pile of silverware on the table. "I'm hungry," she said. "Can we eat now?"

Sweet-Ho nodded. "Everything's ready. Rabble, bring the salad, would you?"

"I'll go if you want me to," Veronica said to her father. She went to the dining room with the silverware.

I carried the bowl of salad to the table. It wasn't heavy, but I felt a great powerful weight inside me.

Later that night, in bed, I felt the feeling again. I didn't cry. I never cry. Not once have I cried since the time that Gnomie died, and even then I wasn't crying for me but for her, that she had to leave her flowers behind before they bloomed, and that there was no way to be right-out absolute-positive that there would be prizewinner delphiniums wherever she was headed.

But the weight came back, inside me, during that time before I went to sleep. And I felt all choky. It was the feeling that things was changing and I couldn't do nothing about it.

11

Norman might come to help," Veronica told me while we walked to Millie Bellows's house on Saturday morning.

I stopped right where I was and stood still, with my arms full of floor wax, the giant can Sweet-Ho had given us. Veronica was carrying a bag of date-and-nut bars that Sweet-Ho had made for Millie, for her sweet tooth.

"When did you talk to Norman Cox?" I asked. "Or did you write him a blackmail letter and not tell me?"

"I didn't even need to," Veronica said. "I sent him a note in school, that I wanted to talk to him, and yesterday afternoon, when you and Sweet-Ho took Gunther to town to buy his new shoes? He called me on the phone."

"Why didn't you tell me?" I demanded.

Veronica looked apologetic. "I didn't have a chance. When you got home, Gunther was showing off his shoes and dancing around, and then Daddy came home and we ate dinner and all. And then afterward, when Gunther was put to bed, we all played Monopoly, remember?"

"Yeah." It was true. Me and Veronica and Sweet-Ho and Mr. Bigelow played a game of Monopoly that lasted so late we was all practically asleep, and even then we just had to quit; no one won.

We started walking again. "Well, did you threaten him about the choir hat? That we'd tell on him?"

Veronica shook her head. "I just told him that we were helping Millie Bellows with her housekeeping, her being so old and not able to keep up, and that we could use some more strong arms for the floors and like that."

"*I'm* strong, Veronica! You didn't need to pretend we was weaklings!" I tried to stick my arm out to make a muscle, but I was lugging this monster can of floor wax, so's I couldn't. Veronica knew about my muscles, anyway.

"Well," she said, "I just thought I'd flatter him. And it worked. He said he'd probably come over and help out this morning."

One part of me could see she was right, and that it *did* work. But shoot, we didn't need him to help with the floor. She missed the whole point, which was to *punish* Norman Cox and force him to make amends. The other part of me got powerfully angry, the first time I ever felt so angry at Veronica.

"Here!" I said all of a sudden. "You think I'm so weak, maybe I shouldn't be carrying this here heavy old floor wax!" I shoved the can at her and grabbed the bag of date-and-nut bars in exchange.

We didn't say anything else but when we got to Millie Bellows's porch, I remembered something and felt sorry for my anger. I remembered that in the afternoon, after lunch, Veronica was going to Meadowhill with her father. I knew how mixed-up she must feel about that because I felt mixed-up about it myself, and shoot, it wasn't even my mother who was crazy.

"Probably he won't even come, dumb old Norman," I said, as we rang the bell and opened the door. Millie liked for us to ring first and then let ourselves in.

But he did. Me and Veronica was barefoot in Millie Bellows's kitchen, hunkered down and scrubbing at that dirty old floor, which probably had never been washed since several husbands ago, when we heard the doorbell ring. Veronica jumped up and almost fell because her feet slid on the soapy floor.

"You don't have to go," I grumbled at her. "It's Millie Bellows's house. Let her answer her own dumb door."

"I have to explain to her about Norman," Veronica said, and rushed out of the kitchen, leaving me scraping away at cruddy stuff by the corner of the refrigerator. I grabbed up a knife from the kitchen table and pried at the sticky old wad of spilled food, pretending it was old Norman Cox and I could just pry him up and throw him away.

109

I could hear them talking in the other room, Veronica and Millie Bellows and Norman. Millie Bellows was quarrelsome as always, complaining that she didn't want that Cox boy in her house, but Veronica was talking all sweet, saying as how we needed his muscles for the heavy work. Next thing I knew, there they were in the kitchen, Veronica and Norman, and Millie was mumbling and shuffling back to her chair in front of the TV.

Just you say one nasty thing, Norman, I thought, glaring at him. Just call me one name, and I'm gone. You can do this old floor your whole self and I don't care none.

But he didn't say nothing. He just stood there, shuffling his old sneakers, while Veronica explained to him about the floor and handed him a scrub brush and a pail of soapy water. Then he knelt down and started in on the corner by the back door.

We worked all morning. Mostly we was pretty silent. Sometimes we'd stand up to dump the dirty water and run fresh from the sink, and to rinse our rags and brushes out.

Sometimes Veronica tried to make conversation. "I declare," she said, all cheerful, "have you ever seen a floor this filthy? I'm amazed she doesn't have cockroaches, aren't you?"

"Probably does, in summer," Norman said.

I didn't even enter into that conversation. I just glared at my corner of the floor and scrubbed at it like I wanted to murder it. Underneath all the dirt, a yellow speckled linoleum was commencing to appear. If

110

me and Veronica was *alone,* like usual, we would've been talking about a million different things, movies and books and school and gossip. But Norman ruined all of that.

"You know what, Norman?" Veronica said, as she rinsed her rags at the sink. "Millie Bellows had a brother named Howard when she was a girl. And when Howard was fourteen, he fell through the ice in the river and was drowned. Isn't that the saddest thing?" She took her rinsed rags back to her bucket and knelt down on the floor again.

Norman grunted something. Then he said, "A deer went through the ice last winter. Right near the edge, down by the Mobil station. Dogs chased him and he ran out on the ice where it was thin."

"Oh, that's a shame," Veronica said. "Deer are so pretty." She moved her bucket and hitched herself across the floor to start on a new place.

"Remember we saw them two does with babies in the meadow last spring?" I said real loud to Veronica. "Like a couple of little Bambis? We oughta go back to that same spot this spring, I bet we'll see some more of them. Let's start out real early in the morning. We can take sandwiches and stuff." I felt this need to start a conversation with Veronica which would leave Norman out and remind him that me and Veronica had all this private stuff we was accustomed to doing together.

But Veronica was doing just the opposite. She was shifting things so they always included Norman. "Do you ever do that, Norman?" she asked, all polite. "Go

111

off outdoors for a whole day, and take your lunch?"

I interrupted so's he wouldn't even have a chance to answer. "Let's do it on a Sunday, Veronica," I said. See, I knew that the Coxes always had to go to church on Sunday morning. "We can take Gunther. I don't believe Gunther's ever had a chance to see a live deer close up, only the ones on them nature shows on TV." I stood up and walked real careful over the wet floor to the sink, to empty my bucket. While the water was running, I said real loud, aiming my voice at Norman, "Our family doesn't go to church so me and Veronica have all this free time on Sunday mornings."

"We go at Easter," Veronica said. "And at Christmas." She was doing it again: saying stuff that would include Norman, and I couldn't figure out why. All of a sudden I hated Veronica.

Millie Bellows interrupted us by coming to the kitchen door and demanding tea. Talk about rude; she could *see* that the kitchen floor was all sloshy and wet and that we was in the middle of hard work on it. But she insisted she wanted tea *right then,* and Veronica got up to put the kettle on. When the tea was ready, I dried my hands and took it in to her. Then I sat there with her and looked at the old photographs for the billionth time. But this time I didn't even listen to her stories about those olden days, nor ask any questions. I was listening to the voices of Norman and Veronica in the kitchen, talking to each other while they scrubbed at the floor.

After a while Veronica came in all smiles, and said

that the floor was done. "Now that it's clean it's the prettiest yellow linoleum, Millie," she said. "And as soon as it's dry, Norman says he'll put the wax on."

"I guess I'll just go on home then," I said, "since you don't need me. I have a lot of stuff to do."

No one said anything. So I stood up and put my jacket on. Before I left, I said in a cool, cruel voice, "Don't be late for lunch, Veronica. Because you and your father have to take that trip this afternoon."

Then I walked home all alone.

I didn't see Veronica and Mr. Bigelow leave for Meadowhill. I heard the car drive away, but I was in Gunther's room getting him cleaned up and dressed to go for an outing with me and Sweet-Ho. That's what Sweet-Ho called it, an outing. "Maybe we'll have us a little outing along the river, Gunther," she said, "and see if we can find us some ducks to feed. We'll take along some bread, how's that? You and me and Rabble, off for an outing."

"Okay," Gunther said. So he didn't even notice that his daddy and Veronica headed off in another direction.

In the other car, the old one that Sweet-Ho used for the shopping and all, we set Gunther up beside Sweet-Ho in his car seat, all buckled in, and opened the window wide beside him. Gunther always got to feeling carsick if the window wasn't open, so we was accustomed to being cold in the car. It was a choice of

113

being cold or having old Gunther throw up, maybe right in your lap.

He sat there in his green corduroy jacket and his green hat with earflaps on, and a plastic bag of bread scraps in his lap.

Sweet-Ho drove real careful down to the road beside the river, and she let Gunther beep the car horn now and then, leaning over from his car seat. Gunther took that responsibility real serious, and only beeped when Sweet-Ho told him he could.

"Daddy lets me sit on his lap and steer," he said, looking over at Sweet-Ho so's she would know it was a question he was asking, though he didn't come right out and ask if he could do it with her.

"Daddy's tall," I explained to him from the back seat, "so it boosts you up when you sit on his lap. But Sweet-Ho's not tall enough for that."

"Oh," Gunther said, nodding his head.

We drove along the river road for some miles and saw plenty of crows and stuff in the trees, but the river was empty and gray. No ducks.

Gunther kept peering out, hiccuping now and then, watching for the ducks and clutching his bundle of bread scraps tight. I felt sorry for his disappointment.

"We should've come last week," I grumbled.

Gunther wiggled around in his seat so's he could look back at me. "They're coming back," he said.

"It sure don't look like it to me, Gun," I told him, trying to let him down easy.

"I don't mean *now*. But sometime. Like people.

People go away, and then they come back. Ducks do, too. They always come back. You have to save up your bread and be ready."

"It's getting too cold, I guess," Sweet-Ho said. "All the ducks went someplace warmer. I expect they're all at Disney World for a vacation." Gunther giggled. He knew she was just joking.

"At Disney World a big Mickey Mouse comes out and shakes your hand," Gunther said. "I saw it on TV. I wouldn't be scared if I went there, would you?"

"Nope," Sweet-Ho said.

"Me neither," I said. "I'd just say, 'How do you do, Mickey?' "

"Do you think we can go there sometime?" Gunther asked.

"Well," Sweet-Ho told him, "we'll have to ask your daddy. Maybe someday we can."

Just when the river started to get boring, since the ducks was all gone, Sweet-Ho told Gunther he could beep once more, and she turned onto another road and we ended up at Fowler's Corners. It's not really a town, just a few houses and a gas station and a little diner. She pulled into the parking lot in front of the diner and said we could go in and get something warm to drink.

"I only want milk," Gunther said.

So when we got settled in a booth and got Gunther's hat off, Sweet-Ho ordered coffee for herself, hot chocolate for me, and a glass of milk for Gunther. It was a pretty nice diner, with shiny Formica tops on the counter and the tables, and on the wall hung a calendar with a real colorful picture of two puppies in a basket. Somebody had written "Debbie loves Brendon forever" with ballpoint pen on the wall beside my seat. On the table there was a sugar jar with one of them tin tops shaped like a volcano.

While the waitress was off getting our order, Gunther announced that he had to go to the bathroom. Sweet-Ho took him, and while she was gone I polished the top of the sugar jar with my fingertip. I could see my face in it, all flattened out and looking something like a prehistoric caveperson. I wished Veronica was there so's she could be a caveperson, too.

The waitress came back while Sweet-Ho and Gunther was gone, and put our things on the table.

"Does your mother take cream?" she asked, and I told her yes, please.

"You look like your mother," the waitress said, as she set down two little paper cups of cream. "Except for your hair color. That sure is pretty hair."

"Thank you. Ginger-colored, it's called," I told her.

"I know a family that has five kids, and every single one of them has bright red hair. But your brother didn't get it, that ginger-color, though, did he?"

"No, he just has that old brown."

"Well, for a boy it don't matter now, does it?" the waitress said, and laid out three paper napkins.

I shook my head. In the back of the diner, I could

see the bathroom door open. Sweet-Ho came out, leaning over to zip Gunther's green jacket.

"My brother and sister both got brown hair," I said. Then I added, real quick, "My sister and my daddy are off on a different outing today."

"That's nice," the waitress said, and then she moved away, smiling at Gunther while Sweet-Ho lifted him back up on the seat of the booth.

"You all have a nice day," the waitress called when we left.

Gunther fell asleep in his car seat while we was driving home, so we didn't have any more horn-beeping. I got sleepy, too, in the backseat, and I closed my eyes and thought about the lie I told the waitress: the lie that Veronica was my sister. If only it was true. I wasn't mad at Veronica anymore, and I wanted my lie to be true.

When we got home, Sweet-Ho carried Gunther into the house and laid him down on the couch. Then she set about making supper, and it was already commencing to get dark outside when Mr. Bigelow and Veronica got back.

Veronica ran upstairs to change her clothes — her daddy made her wear a dress to the hospital — and I followed her and went into her room. "I brought you this," I said. "Me and Gunther and Sweet-Ho went for an outing and we stopped at a diner." I gave her two little toothpicks with fringed paper on their ends which I took from a box beside the cash register at the diner.

"Thanks." She took them and stuck them into a corner of her mirror frame, next to one of the Halloween snapshots. "I thought you were mad at me."

"Not anymore."

She zipped up her jeans and started looking around for a shirt. "I couldn't bring you anything because we didn't stop anyplace."

"Not even for a Pepsi or nothing?"

Veronica pulled a sweatshirt over her head and then grabbed her ponytail through. "There was this lounge at the hospital and we had a drink there, from a machine. I had to have grape because it was all out of everything else."

"Is that all you did, just sat and had grape?" I felt funny asking about her visit to the hospital.

"We walked around some, outside. They have benches and stuff. We sat on a bench and talked."

"What did you talk about?" I couldn't remember Mrs. Bigelow talking much, ever. Just smiling.

"The weather. And Daddy told her about Gunther wearing my ballerina costume. He made it into a funny story. We didn't tell her about Millie Bellows getting hit by the stone, of course. Just about Gunther dancing."

"Did she laugh?"

Veronica shook her head. She sat down on the bed to tie her sneakers. "No. She just kept watching while we talked. She didn't say much, just nodded her head. And her hair looked horrible, like she doesn't comb it."

118

"After you walked around, then you just got back in the car to come home?"

"No, then she — my mother — went back to where she stays. A nurse took her. And Daddy went off in a room to talk to the doctors. I had to wait in the lounge. I read a bunch of old *Good Housekeeping*s."

"What did the doctors say? Did he tell you?"

"Just that she has a lot of medication, and it makes her walk slow and not talk much. And they said she's getting better."

It didn't sound better to me, not combing her hair and not talking. Before, she always kept her hair nice, at least. But I didn't say that to Veronica. "Was it fun, going there?" I asked her.

"No. I hated it."

"I wish you could've gone with us. We looked for ducks on the river, and Sweet-Ho let Gunther beep the car horn."

Mr. Bigelow called from the foot of the stairs. "Girls! Time to set the table!"

"Thanks for the toothpicks," Veronica said as we headed down the hall.

"I told the waitress they was for my sister," I said, and Veronica grinned.

12

Mr. Bigelow gave Gunther his bath while me and Veronica helped Sweet-Ho with the dishes. Then he brought him downstairs in his pj's, with his hair all slicked down and ointment rubbed on his eczema.

Gunther climbed onto the couch with an armload of books, to get his bedtime story.

"Daddy," he asked, "will you take us to Disney World? A big Mickey Mouse comes out and shakes your hand. Sweet-Ho told me to ask if you would take us."

Sweet-Ho came out of the kitchen, laughing and wiping her hands on a towel. "Hold it, Gunther," she said. "Phil, I just told him he'd have to ask his daddy, that's all."

Mr. Bigelow scooped Gunther up onto his lap and turned on the lamp beside the couch. "Tell you what, Big Gun. If I ever sell the Rockwell house, I'll take all of us to Disney World for a whole week. How's that?"

"Okay," Gunther said, and reached for a book.

I looked over at Veronica. Me and Veronica had a secret about the Rockwell house. It was an enormous house set up high on a hill on the side of town, and it had towers and porches sticking out every which way. Nobody had lived in it for as long as I could remember. It looked even more neglected than Millie Bellows's little house, but you could picture how, with new paint and the windows fixed, and all them acres of lawn mowed, it would be like a mansion. Veronica and me planned to buy it when we grew up. We was going to live there together and take in all the orphans we could find. If we had children of our own, of course they would live there, too. In all of them bedrooms there was going to be zillions of cribs and little beds, and we would have one big room full of nothing but toys, and outside there would be swings and see-saws and such.

We would have to hire people to help look after them, of course, but we already figured out how we was going to find them in special places, not just advertising in the dumb old Highriver newspaper where people advertise for clerks and computer technicians. We plotted this out real careful. We was planning to find out where they make those greeting cards, those kind that say, "To a Special Little Boy Who's 2 Today." Hallmark and like that. Then we would go there, to that card factory, and maybe stand out by the gate, like politicians shaking hands at a factory gate, and we'd hand out leaflets. That way all the people who write them cards? Like the lady who wrote this one, which came to Gunther from his grandma in Tennessee on Easter:

> *Here's a bunny who hopped your way*
> *And a froggie, come to play*
> *With a special boy so far away*
> *On this Happy Easter Day!*

Veronica and me, we figured out that all them ladies in card factories would be the ones we want to work in our orphans home. So we'd offer to pay them more, and give them lots of benefits and such. But the real benefit would be that instead of making up those little poems and thinking about little children far away, they could be right there *with* the little children, caring for them and hugging them all the time.

And here's the real clever thing that Veronica thought up. You know how most ads say "Experience essential"? Or "Minimum two years experience"? Well, our leaflet would say:

> *Experience not required.*
> *Only LOVE desired.*

It was Veronica's idea to make it in rhyme so's it would stand out on the page.

That was our dream, Veronica's and mine, to fill that house up with little orphans and with Hallmark ladies. Her and me would live there too. Sweet-Ho, if she wanted. And Gunther could.

It wouldn't be the Rockwell house anymore after

that. Down at the end of the driveway, there would be a sign, not neon or nothing, but one of them white signs with black letters like you see at the gate to a horse farm. And it would say: THE VERONICA PARABLE HOME.

I thought about that while Mr. Bigelow read *Mike Mulligan and His Steam Shovel* to Gunther. I expect Veronica was thinking about it, too.

When Sweet-Ho was upstairs putting Gunther to bed, Mr. Bigelow gave a big stretch of his arms and said, "I'm bushed."

"Tired," Veronica said.

"Exhausted," I said.

"Fatigued," Mr. Bigelow said.

"Pooped," Veronica said.

"Wait a minute," I said, and I ran up the stairs to my room to get the thesaurus. "Weary!" Mr. Bigelow called up the stairs after me.

After I looked it up in the thesaurus, I added, "Prostrate." Then I gave the book to Veronica, and she said, "Spent."

By the time Sweet-Ho had come back down, we had made up the rules of a game. One person chose a word and got to hold the thesaurus. Then the rest of us thought up other words for it in turn, and the one who got the most — they had to be listed in the thesaurus — was the winner of that round.

Veronica took the book and announced: "Untruth!"

I got to go first and I said, "Lie." That was easy. So I got a point.

Then Mr. Bigelow said, "Fib," and got a point.

Sweet-Ho said, "Falsehood," so we were even, one point for each, and it was my turn again.

Shoot, I couldn't think of nothing. Finally I had to pass.

Mr. Bigelow was stuck for a minute, too, but finally he said, "Invention? I seem to remember I had a teacher in school who used to say, 'That's quite an invention' if somebody told a lie."

Veronica moved her finger along the page of words, and found it. "Invention. Two points for you, Daddy. Your turn, Sweet-Ho."

"Fabrication," Sweet-Ho said, quick as anything. Two points for her. And I had to pass again.

Then Mr. Bigelow passed.

"You and Daddy are tied, Sweet-Ho," Veronica said.

Sweet-Ho grinned. "Misrepresentation," she said, and won that round.

Mr. Bigelow took the thesaurus and searched for a word while Sweet-Ho went out to the kitchen and got a pitcher of lemonade and four glasses on a tray. When she got back, we played again. Mr. Bigelow's word was "white" — and shoot, Sweet-Ho won again. Me and Veronica got things like "ivory" and "creamy," but Sweet-Ho, she kept going and said words I never heard of, like "alabaster," and before we knew it, she won again.

And the next time, and the next. Sweet-Ho won every single time, even beating out Mr. Bigelow on business-type words. She was kind of embarrassed, winning every round, but you could tell she was pleased, too.

We all looked at her, amazed, after we quit the game and put the book down on the table. "I read a lot," she said, explaining why she won.

"Have you ever thought about going to college, Sweet-Ho?" Mr. Bigelow asked.

She busted out laughing. "I never went past eighth grade," she said. "One thing I always wished was that I finished school. Don't you ever even *consider* quitting school, Rabble, or I swear I'll take a stick to your backside." She was joking about the stick, I knew. But she spoke real fierce.

"Wait a minute," Mr. Bigelow said, serious-like. "You could, Sweet-Ho. The community college gives extension courses in the evenings. I don't think you have to have a high school diploma. If you did, it would be easy enough for you to take the equivalency test."

But Sweet-Ho just kept laughing, all embarrassed. "I get all nervous even thinking about a test," she said. "You know I was *shaking* when I took my driver's test?"

Me and Veronica took the tray of glasses and the pitcher out to the kitchen. It was bedtime. Sweet-Ho and Mr. Bigelow said good night, and we went upstairs. From the bedroom, while I put on my nightgown, I could hear them talking. I could hear that Sweet-Ho was still laughing and protesting, and that Mr. Bigelow, in his deep, quiet voice, was explaining about the college courses and reassuring her.

Later, when she came up, I was still awake. While she brushed her hair in the darkness, with only a little light coming in from the hall through the partly open door, I watched her from my bed.

"Phil says that they have all these courses in literature," she said to me. "Like poetry and novels and drama. You remember, Rabble, when we went to see that play where the little girl and her friend hung out in the kitchen all the time, with the cook? Remember that? And she had her hair all chopped off like a boy? Wasn't that something? What was it called?"

Member of the Wedding, I told her.

She nodded her head and brushed her hair some more, looking at herself in the mirror in the dim light. "That's right. *Member of the Wedding*. I thought about that play for the longest time afterward. Just to see them moving about and speaking, on the stage, as if they were in real life. Wasn't that something, though?"

"Mmmmmm."

"I surely would love to *learn* about those things," Sweet-Ho said softly, almost to herself. "But I know I'd be too scared."

"Only at first," I told her. "At first you'd be scared, but then after a while, it'd be okay. After you got used to it."

She sighed and went to the dresser for her nightgown. "It takes me so long to get used to things, Rabble," she said.

❉   ❉   ❉

Mr. Bigelow, once he got an idea, never let go of it, not if it was a good idea. For example, once, a couple of years ago, he started getting after Veronica for biting her fingernails. First he just lectured her a bit, saying as how it made her hands look ugly, which was true, but that didn't seem to work on her, because she had the habit already and couldn't break herself of it, even though she wanted pretty hands. Most people would just give up after that. But Mr. Bigelow, he went down to Woolworth and came back with a little bag filled with fingernail stuff. I was some astounded that a *man* would go right in there to the cosmetics counter and buy that stuff, but he wasn't even embarrassed or nothing. He laid it all out on the kitchen table for Veronica: nail files and little brushes and tools for keeping your hands nice, and the best part was three bottles of polish — one pink, and one bright red, and one real special, glittery silver.

And he told her she could use the polish, even could wear it to *school,* once she got her hands looking nice. She could even wear the *silver* to school if she wanted, he said, though she may not want to look that fancied-up in fourth grade.

And it worked. After that, if she started in to bite her nails, she had only to be reminded in a nice way of all those fancy polishes, waiting for proper hands to put them on. By the time a couple of months had passed, she had normal-looking fingernails, and her daddy made a big celebration of it, and he even helped her paint them pink.

After a little while she didn't wear the polish to

school no more, just kept it in her room to fool with on weekends. But her nails stayed nice.

And once when Gunther just couldn't keep from scratching at his old eczema, Mr. Bigelow got him a giant box of Band-Aids, the kind with stars and hearts in different colors, and stuck them on Gunther's arms in the places Gunther chose, to remind him not to scratch.

I always think on that nail polish celebration, and the Band-Aids, when I need to remember that the best way to get people to change their ways, or change their minds, is to treat them nice about it.

It was the same thing Mr. Bigelow began to do with Sweet-Ho. First he came home from work one evening with some catalogues, and said he had just happened along past the college building where they had these out on a table, and he thought she might like to read through them sometime. One of the catalogues described all the evening courses, and sure enough, they were like he had said: courses teaching about poetry and plays and such. And there were other courses, too.

We read about them out loud at dinner. "Here's one for you, Gunther," Mr. Bigelow said, and then read a whole paragraph about Biochemistry, which sounded like the most mystifying thing in the entire world. We all laughed and hooted.

"My turn!" Veronica said, and took the book. She read about Accounting Procedures, and we all made faces.

Sweet-Ho read about the course in the art department called Intermediate Ceramics, and we all busted out laughing when she got to the part in the description where it said, "pot-throwing."

"We could do that right here at home," Mr. Bigelow said. "We could just open up the kitchen cupboard and throw pots all over the house."

"Don't you dare," Sweet-Ho said sternly.

When it was my turn, I found the one called Introduction to American Literature, and read about that. At the end of the paragraph it said, "Included in the semester's reading will be Hawthorne's *The Scarlet Letter*, Twain's *Huckleberry Finn*, Steinbeck's *The Grapes of Wrath*, and —"

Sweet-Ho interrupted me. "Does it really say that, Rabble? *The Grapes of Wrath?*"

I leaned over and showed her, on the page.

She looked up all amazed, when she realized I didn't make it up. "I already read that," she said. "I read it on my own, from the library. I believe it's the most wonderful book I ever read."

She took the catalogue from me and peered at the page again. "But I can't think what they might *teach* you about it. Wouldn't reading it be enough? Look here, it says: characterization, theme, plot structure. I don't even know what that means. You think if they taught you about that stuff, then you could read a book again, and you could enjoy it even *more?* I don't see how that could be."

She closed up the catalogue, shaking her head, all

puzzled. Later in the evening, while we was all watching TV, I saw her reach over and pick it up again and turn to that page. She still had it in her lap when I went to kiss her good night, and that night she stayed downstairs till late.

13

A couple of nights later, Mr. Bigelow brought a book home. At first I thought it was from the library because it was a real hardcover book, not just a paperback like we buy all the time down at Highriver Cards and Books. And also it wasn't new. You could tell it had been read a whole lot already.

"I had to go to Clarksburg on business today," he said, "and I saw a secondhand bookstore. So I went in to browse around, and I found this. I thought I might read you one of the stories in it. It's one I remember from when I was younger."

"Does it have pictures?" Gunther asked, but his daddy said no.

"Well, that's okay," Gunther said.

Sweet-Ho peered over to see the cover. "Steinbeck?" she said. "That's the same one who wrote *The Grapes of Wrath*, right?"

Mr. Bigelow nodded.

"Well, I surely did like *The Grapes of Wrath*," Sweet-Ho said. "I expect I'd like any story Mr. Steinbeck wrote."

That night after supper, Mr. Bigelow settled himself down in his big chair, with Gunther curled up like a pretzel in his lap and the rest of us close by. He turned through the pages until he found the story he remembered from when he was younger.

"*The Red Pony*," he read. "That's the title."

Gunther gave a sigh. "I love ponies," he said.

Next Mr. Bigelow read, " 'The Gift.' " He explained, "That's the name of the first part of the story."

Gunther sighed again. "I love gifts, too," he said.

Then Mr. Bigelow began the story. " 'At daybreak Billy Buck emerged from the bunkhouse and stood for a moment on the porch looking up at the sky . . .' "

Right away I could see it, clear as anything, in my mind. I could see Billy Buck, and then when he got to the boy, Jody, I could see him, too. Jody was littler than Veronica and me and needed a haircut. I could see Jody's daddy, all stern. And I could see them two dogs they had, with their foolish names — Doubletree Mutt and Smasher. Gunther surely did grin at those names. We all did.

While Mr. Bigelow read, I could hardly take my eyes from him, and from the book in his hands. But when he paused for a moment and leaned over to take a sip from the cup of coffee on the table beside him, I

looked around and could see that we was all —
Gunther and Veronica and Sweet-Ho, as well as
me — we was all waiting, barely breathing, for him to
go on.

I knew that each one of us could see it in our own
minds. And probably we saw different things. A book
with no pictures lets you make your own pictures in
your mind. A guy who writes a book like that really
trusts the people who read it to make the kind of pictures he wants them to. Of course he helps them along
with the words. Like Mr. Steinbeck told us all about
that old dog named Smasher having only one ear because the other got bit off by a coyote, and how his
one good ear stood up higher than the ear on a regular
collie. So we could all picture Smasher in our minds,
just the way he was supposed to be, but at the same
time each of us had our own private Smasher, built
out of all the dogs we had ever known.

Mr. Bigelow read on and on, sipping at his coffee
now and then, and usually Sweet-Ho would have
asked him if he wanted his coffee heated up. But she
didn't say nothing. It would have been wrong to in-
terrupt a story like that, which just flowed along like
the creek in spring, pounding hard and full of grit
against the rocky, dangerous places, flattening out all
smooth and clear and fine here and there, but always
moving moving moving.

And oh lord, some parts of it was exciting, and some
was sad, and some scary. Now and again I could
scarcely breathe, waiting for what came next.

Finally he stopped.

"That's the end of the first section," he said.

"Read more," Veronica begged. "Please."

But he said, "Not tonight. It's late. I'll start the next part tomorrow night."

"What's the next part called?" Gunther asked, peering into the book as if he could read.

His daddy looked down at the page. " 'The Great Mountains'," he told us.

In the morning, me and Veronica talked about it on the way to school. "I almost burst out crying," Veronica said. "Remember that part when the pony —"

"Shhh," I said. "I can't even talk about that part."

She nodded. "Yeah. Do you think it will get sadder?"

"I don't see as how it could. Anyways, the next part's called 'The Great Mountains', remember? That don't sound sad."

She corrected me. "Doesn't. No, it doesn't sound sad. Maybe —" Veronica began, but she got interrupted by Diane Briggs, who came running up to us as we got near to school.

"Rabble! Veronica!" Diane said, all excited. "Guess what! I'm going to have a boy-girl party! Next Saturday, for my birthday!"

Some other girls in our class came up, too, and we all started talking about the party. Nobody had ever had a boy-girl party up till now. Most birthday parties was just a bunch of girls going to the movies together, with McDonald's afterward, and the birthday person's mother paid for everything.

"Each of you has to invite a boy," Diane said. "It's at my house, and we'll have pizza, and I can rent any movie I want for the VCR. Not X-rated, of course. I think I'm going to get *The Karate Kid.*"

They all started talking and laughing about who they might invite. Not me, though. I didn't like the idea much. What if you asked some boy and he said no? Just thinking about it made me feel funny.

In school I looked around the classroom at the different boys. I knew Veronica would ask Norman Cox, especially now that he was helping us at Millie Bellows's house. She already forgave him for the stone-throwing and all, since she figured out it was because he liked her and wanted to draw her attention. And I knew who each of them other girls would ask, because they each had someone they liked special.

I just sat there all gloomy through silent reading, even though it was usually my favorite part of school. I kept looking up from my book, thinking how it would be to ask a boy, what he might say, how he might act. After a while I noticed that my thoughts kept coming back to old Parker Condon, and I knew it would have to be him I asked.

Parker Condon was practically the only boy in sixth grade who never acted rude. Once or twice him and me was on a project together, and he was always helpful and stuff, and sometimes I borrowed his marking pens when we did maps. Veronica said Parker liked me, and I guess I knew it was true.

He wasn't good-looking. He was too skinny and his hair stuck up funny in the back, like maybe he slept on it wrong. And he was nervous and shy.

Me, all of a sudden *I* felt nervous and shy myself at the idea of asking Parker Condon to a party. I could feel my face going hot and pink, just thinking about it.

I began to plan how I could say, all casual-like, "You probably don't want to go to Diane's party with me, do you?" Then if he said no, I could pretend like I already knew he didn't want to. I could just laugh and shrug my shoulders and all like that, like the whole idea was stupid anyways.

Then I thought maybe I could call him on the telephone so's he couldn't see my face when I asked.

At morning recess, I made Veronica come over in a corner so we could talk private, and I told her I was going to ask Parker Condon but I didn't know how.

"Look," she said, and she pulled a piece of notebook paper out of the pocket of her jeans. "I wrote this during math."

I unfolded it and read the note she had written to Norman Cox. It was real short. It just said, "Diane's having a boy-girl party Saturday for her birthday. Do you want to go?"

I asked her could I copy it, and she said sure. After I did, I put my own note in my own pocket and carried it around with me all day.

"I gave Norman my note during lunch," Veronica

told me right after school when we was walking home. "But he didn't answer it yet. Did you give yours to Parker?"

I shook my head. It was still all folded in my pocket.

"Well, there he is." Veronica pointed. There was Parker Condon, across the street, walking home. His hair was all sticking up spiky and stupid, and his sweatshirt was too big. I started thinking maybe I should ask someone else. Or maybe I shouldn't ask no one. Maybe I should just stay home on Saturday.

Veronica poked me. "Give it to him," she said.

"You stay with me," I told her. "Promise?"

Veronica promised, and we crossed the street to where Parker was.

"Hi," he said, all nervous, when he saw us.

"Hi, Parker," Veronica said. "Rabble has something for you."

Well, then there was nothing I could do but dig into my pocket and pull out the note. I poked it at him. "It's a note," I said. "You don't need to read it till you get home."

He didn't say nothing. He put it into his pocket and looked at the ground. "I gotta go," he said after a minute.

Veronica and I turned and ran. We started laughing as we ran toward home. Running and laughing, I remembered how, in the story, the boy Jody sat in the saddle put over a sawhorse, and pretended like he was riding on a real horse. How, in his mind, he could see the fields go flying by, and hear the beat of the galloping hoofs.

Each night Mr. Bigelow read a part of *The Red Pony.* There was four parts altogether, and the third was the best. Each night we all sat there silent while he read, even Gunther, though he probably couldn't understand lots of the words. Each night I went to bed without saying much, just thinking on the story, just remembering each thing that happened in it. Each night Sweet-Ho sat up late, and once when I peered over the banister I could see her there in the chair, turning the book over and over in her hands.

When he was finished, on the fourth night, and closed the book, Gunther said what I felt.

"Read it again, Daddy," Gunther said.

Mr. Bigelow smiled and kissed him on the back of his neck, between where his sleeper suit ended and his shaggy hair began, right there where it was pink and smooth.

"Someday I will," his daddy said. Gunther sighed.

Me and Veronica was planning what we would wear to Diane's party on Saturday. Parker Condon had said yes. Well, he didn't really say yes, but he sent back my note during math, and on the bottom he had put "OK" in big letters with a square drawn around them, all of it in ballpoint pen. You could see where he had first wrote it in pencil and then drawn over it in pen real careful.

Stupid old Norman Cox had said yes, too, but not

tasteful in a note like Parker. He had just said it right out, at Millie Bellows's house while he was painting the dirty old woodwork in the kitchen, and me and Veronica was cleaning out the cupboards.

"Do I have to bring a present?" he asked.

"Well, of course," Veronica told him. "It's her birthday."

"I don't know what to get a girl," Norman grumbled.

"Diane likes to draw," Veronica reminded him. "You could get her a set of markers or something."

"Yeah, I guess. Or paints maybe. You want to go in on it with me so we could get something more expensive?"

I almost held my breath. I stood there with a stack of plates in my hand, waiting to hear what Veronica would say. Me and her had already planned to go in together on a big bottle of cologne that we saw down at the drugstore.

"That's a good idea, Norman," Veronica said, "but Rabble and I are already planning to do that."

"Yeah, okay," Norman said, and dipped his brush back in the can of white paint.

I felt so relieved that I was able to be nice to Norman all of a sudden. "They have real nice art supplies down at the hardware store," I told him. "Books on how to draw and everything, too, back in the corner behind the kitchen stuff."

In Veronica's room, every night, after we went upstairs, we tried on her dresses. She had dressier ones than me, and she said I could borrow any one I chose.

139

She was taller but she had some that fit me, some she had outgrown, still hanging there. On Thursday night, Mr. Bigelow knocked and poked his head in the door when he heard us giggling in there. When he looked in, I was wearing a yellow dress that was kind of babyish because it was two years old. But it fit good. Veronica was holding up two others on hangers, trying to decide between them.

Mr. Bigelow said some admiring stuff about how I looked in the yellow dress, not pointing out that it was babyish. Maybe he didn't notice.

Then he said, "Actually, I was kind of hoping that all of your clothes would be too small, Veronica. Yours too, Rabble. I was kind of hoping that I could take the two of you shopping tomorrow evening for new party dresses at the mall."

"We both *have* grown a lot, Daddy," Veronica said, grinning.

"I can see that. How about it? Is it a date, tomorrow night after supper?"

"Sure," Veronica said.

He looked at me. "Rabble?"

"You really mean me, too?" I could hardly believe it.

"I have an overwhelming urge to buy two new dresses for my two best girls," he said, "for their first boy-girl party."

The next night, after supper, he took me and Veronica in the car to the mall. Sweet-Ho had cautioned me, though she didn't need to, about how I shouldn't take forever making up my mind the way I usually do. How I should be grateful for whatever Mr. Bigelow decided on, even if it might be something I didn't like much. How I should veer away from anything that might cost a whole lot.

Shoot, I would've done that anyway, without her reminding me. I would've worn Veronica's old babyish yellow dress with the puffy sleeves and all, without complaining.

He took us right to a big old department store, where toward the back they had a whole section called "Hoyden." I didn't know what that meant and neither did the saleslady; I asked her, and she just shrugged, so I made up my mind to look it up when I got back home. Mr. Bigelow didn't know neither, but he said somebody in his office had told him it was the place to come.

Then he sat down in a chair in the "Hoyden" department, not even minding that he was the only man in sight, and he told me and Veronica we could pick what we wanted and try it on.

Oh lord, it was something. We skipped right past the jeans and all, and went to where there was racks and racks of dresses, and each one was better than the one before.

"Look," I whispered to Veronica, and held out the skirt of a red dress with little white flowers all over.

She nodded. "Why don't you try it on?" she said back.

But the saleslady came over. She was gray-haired, like maybe she was somebody's grandmother, and she had a nice smile. "You know," she said to me, "when

141

you came in, I noticed your beautiful hair and those green eyes. I think you might want to look at the greens, to match those eyes."

Shoot, I hadn't even gotten to the greens yet, I was so caught up with that red. But when she said that, I moved over to where the greens was hanging farther down, figuring she was a clothes expert and all and might be right. And there was the same dress, the same little white flowers all over it and the same big white collar. But this one was green, and it looked like a meadow in spring, the meadow that I remembered right behind my Gnomie's house, just as those earliest white flowers blossomed.

"I think this would be your size," the lady said, and lifted one out from the rack. "Let's hold it up." She held the dress against me, in front of a mirror, and I could see she was right about the green. My eyes peered back at me above that dress, and even though my jeans and sneakers was sticking out at the bottom, it didn't matter. I could see that the green dress was the perfect one.

I waited while Veronica chose, because I didn't want to go into the dressing room all alone. I didn't know if the lady would go in with us or what, and it made me sort of embarrassed.

Finally Veronica picked out a blue dress, an old-timey style with little pearl buttons up to the neck, where there was a tiny ruffle.

And after that we didn't even need to look anymore, or to spend time thinking or deciding. We tried them on, together in a little dressing room with mir-

142

rors all around, while the woman waited outside. Then when we said we was ready, she came in and smoothed the material over our shoulders and did the button that I missed in the middle of my back.

"Well, I don't know which one of you looks more beautiful," she said. "Won't your daddy be pleased? You go right on out there and show him."

When we did, Mr. Bigelow got a smile on his face that widened and widened. Veronica posed and turned around like a model, but I felt too shy. I just stood there in the green dress, hoping my posture was good.

He looked at the tags that hung down from our sleeves, and I got nervous because I hadn't remembered to look at the price and make sure that I didn't pick an expensive one. But I guess not, because he nodded to the lady and told her that the dresses would be just fine.

"Unless you want to try on some others?" he said to us.

But we both shook our heads. Once you put on the perfect dress you don't want to try on something else and get your thinking all confused. There's no need.

She put them in separate boxes so's we could each carry our own, going home.

Back at the house, we modeled them again, for Sweet-Ho and Gunther, and this time we changed out of our sneakers and put on our good shoes, and this time I didn't feel so foolish about my posture and all, so I was able to walk and twirl like Veronica did.

Gunther, setting there on Sweet-Ho's lap in his pj's,

143

all ready for bed, clapped his hands like we was a show or something. He commenced to sing in a Kermit the Frog voice, " 'It's not easy being green . . .' "

We all laughed. It *was* easy being green, at least in that beautiful green-meadow dress.

I saw the dictionary there on Mr. Bigelow's desk, and I picked it up and leafed through to the H pages.

" 'Hoyden,' " I read out loud. "That's what the part of the store was called," I explained to Sweet-Ho. "The part where we got the dresses.

" 'Hoyden. Bold girl,' " I read. I liked that. Standing there in the green flowered dress, feeling beautiful, I suddenly took a mind to do a thing that only a truly bold girl would do.

I went over to Mr. Bigelow and put my arms around him and gave him a big hug.

14

We was all, girls and boys, supposed to meet at the party. Sweet-Ho drove me and Veronica. It isn't far to Diane's house, just down past the grocery store and over a couple of streets. But Sweet-Ho could tell we felt embarrassed, walking in our new dresses and carrying our present, the big bottle of cologne all wrapped up, with two different birthday cards.

It feels okay just to be walking along in jeans, maybe carrying schoolbooks. But walking all dressed up, and with our hair washed and curled and all — well, what if someone from school saw us, maybe someone who wasn't invited, and if they made fun?

Sweet-Ho pretended like she had to go to the store right then, and said since she was going anyway, in the car, why didn't she give us a ride to Diane's house? So we pretended like we really thought she needed groceries and said sure, we might as well keep her company in the car, even though we all of us knew that Diane's house was three blocks out of her way.

Parker Condon's dad was just dropping him off, too, when we got there. I glanced over at him, playing like I was just looking over to admire the Briggses' mailbox, which was one of them mailboxes with pheasants painted on it. Somehow Parker had managed to slick down them spikes of hair that usually stick up in the back like insect feelers. And he was carrying his present in a brown paper bag; I could sympathize with that, because it must be even more embarrassing for a boy to carry a fancy, wrapped-up present.

Veronica said hi to Parker, but I pretended like I didn't notice him, like I was all interested in that pheasanty mailbox.

Then Norman Cox rode up on his bike, and lord, he was all gussied up, too. That very morning we was with him at Millie Bellows's house, and he was same as always, wearing a grubby shirt and foul sneakers while he pruned the bushes in her yard. Now, at two o'clock, he had on clean clothes and regular shoes, like he was going to church or something. He looked as if he had even had a bath. His hair had a part in it.

He leaned his bike against the side of the Briggses' garage and we all of us went up to ring the doorbell.

Most of the other people was already there, and it was strange inside. Everybody was just sitting there all dressed up, in the Briggses' family room: all the boys on one side, and all the girls on the other, and presents piled up on the Ping-Pong table, and all of us not looking over that way, pretending the presents wasn't there. Nobody was talking much. It was like we was all strangers in a Greyhound station or something.

Mrs. Briggs kept coming in and passing stuff like Cokes and popcorn around. She commented nicely on all our dresses, and said polite stuff like "How's your family?" We all cringed when she asked Corrine Foster whether her mother had had her baby yet, and Corrine said no, not yet, and blushed.

Finally Mrs. Briggs said, "Why don't you open all these lovely gifts, Diane?" so's we had to stop pretending the pile of presents wasn't there.

You could tell that mothers had bought the boys' gifts. Well, maybe not Norman, because he had brought just what we had suggested, some art supplies in a paper bag from the hardware store, not even wrapped up, but Diane was some pleased. She said she didn't have any markers that good. We all tried out the markers, writing our names in different colors on the paper bag. Parker wrote his name in lime green, right under my purple.

But the other boys had all brought presents wrapped in decorated paper, with bows made out of curly ribbon. One was a book, and one was a hair-brush-and-comb set, and one was some stationery that had a cartoon of a guy with a saxophone and said "Just a note" under it.

Diane squirted all of the girls with the cologne me and Veronica brought, and then she tried to squirt the boys, but they all acted real macho and shoved her away. After that everybody started talking a little more.

Next Mrs. Briggs put the movie into the VCR and set out a big bowl of popcorn, and we all sat down again, still boys on one side and girls on the other. Everybody had already seen *The Karate Kid* — Norman said he seen it twice — so we knew what was going to happen, and that made it better. We all yelled and cheered and stuff. When it ended, we all did karate moves, yelling "Hhhaaaaa" the way they do. And foolish old Parker Condon took the scarf that somebody gave Diane as a present, tied it around his waist like a black belt, and came at me with his hand made into a weapon aimed at my middle, so's I fell into a fit of giggling.

When we started sitting down again, everybody was rearranged, so now boys was sitting next to girls all of a sudden, as if by accident. Some of us — me for one — had birthday wrapping ribbons tied around our foreheads like sweatbands for karate.

Mrs. Briggs had come in during the movie and put a big paper tablecloth on the Ping-Pong table, and set up folding chairs around. Now she put Cokes at each place, and paper plates, and finally she brought in two big, loaded pizzas and told us it was time to eat. When we went to the table, we all just sat down girl-boy-girl-boy as if it was natural.

I noticed that Parker, sitting next to me, smelled like sweat. But I couldn't fault him none for that because of the karate moves that required a lot of jumping around. I just hoped I didn't smell like sweat. But I figured that the cologne would cover it up if I did.

Nobody liked anchovies, not a single person, except Diane. So we piled all the anchovies on a paper plate and sent them up to Diane at the end of the table, for an extra birthday present. Then we got the idea to pile all the mushrooms on another plate, and all the pepperonis on another, and all the green peppers, and like that. We fooled around a lot with them pizzas and didn't really eat much, to tell the truth. But it was fun.

"You know what Jeff did once when he was little?" Peter Hardesty said. "He went out in the woods and picked a whole bunch of mushrooms and brought them home for his mother. But half of what he picked was *poison!* Good thing his mother knew to throw them all away!"

Jeff Murphy, sitting up at the end of the table beside Diane — he was the boy she invited — got all embarrassed. "I was only five when I did that," he explained. "Anyway, Peter, I know something *you* did once. You guys wanta hear what Peter did?"

We all called out, "Yeah!" So Jeff told about when all the guys was at Boy Scout camp together a couple of years ago, and when one of the counselors was in the outhouse Peter nailed the door shut on him, so he couldn't get out and had to yell for help, and Peter got into trouble. When Jeff was telling it, Peter kept pretending to hate it, but you could tell he was some proud for having thought of a trick like that.

When we quit laughing, Diane swallowed the last

anchovy and announced, "I got an idea for a game! We'll go around the table, and everybody gets a turn. And you have to tell some secret you know about somebody else at the table, okay?"

"You go first, Diane!" Veronica said.

Diane started in laughing. "Okay. I'll tell on Corrine!"

"No fair!" Corrine Foster yelled.

"You'll get your turn, Corrine," Diane said. "Anyway, this isn't so bad. One time Corrine and I were at the mall, just fooling around, and we were in that store that sells jeans and T-shirts, you know the one?"

We all nodded. "Jeaneology, it's called," Veronica said. "Is that the one you mean?"

"Oh, don't tell about that!" Corrine giggled, and covered her face with her hands.

"Yeah, that's the one," Diane went on. "And when we started to go out, this alarm sounded, real loud."

"What'd it sound like?" someone asked.

Diane did a sound like a real loud buzzer.

"What'd you do?"

"Well, I was already outside," Diane went on, "but Corrine was standing there in the door, scared to move, and this alarm kept going. And a clerk came over to her, all stern, and took her by the arm."

"Then what?"

"He took her back in the store, so I followed behind, and when they got her to the counter where the cash register is, we could all see that there was a belt caught on her sweater. It was just hanging there, she didn't even know it was there. But the tag was still

150

attached, of course, so it made the shoplifting alarm go off."

"Did they call the police?"

Corrine looked up, finally, and took her hands away from her face. "I've never been so embarrassed," she said. "Everybody was looking."

"Well, they believed her," Diane said, "because of the way the belt was caught. If she'd wanted to steal it, she wouldn't hang it there on her sweater right where you could see it. So they let her go."

"Lucky," someone said.

Now Corrine was laughing, now that the story was all told.

"And also," Diane added, "Corrine was crying."

Corrine stopped laughing. "That's not fair, Diane! You didn't have to tell that!"

Diane shrugged. "Well," she said, "it's true." She looked around. "You already did one, Jeff. So it's your turn, Veronica."

I got all nervous because I knew the one Veronica would tell on was *me*. And Veronica knew all my secrets, every one. I looked at her, and she was grinning. "Let me think," she said. "I guess I'll tell one on Rabble."

Everyone yelled and pointed at me. I looked down at the plate of pepperonis in front of me. I waited, all nervous.

"Once upon a time," Veronica began, all dramatic-like, and everyone groaned. She started again. "Once upon a time, when Rabble was about nine years old, she found this old dried-up hornet's nest in the garage

151

at the end of the summer. And she thought it was pretty; you know how nature-loving Rabble is?"

Everybody said "Yeah," and I relaxed, because I knew what Veronica was going to tell, and it wasn't so bad. I felt a whole lot of gratitude to her, considering all the things she *could've* told on me.

"So she brought it inside for her mother," Veronica went on, "and put it right in the middle of their kitchen table, like for a centerpiece?"

"I bet hornets came out, didn't they?" Parker asked.

"Yeah," Veronica said. "All these mad hornets came out and Rabble got stung right on her butt!"

Everybody shrieked with laughter. Except me, of course. She didn't need to tell *that* part. I got stung on my elbow, too, and she didn't even *mention* that.

Well, lord, we went round the table and everybody had a story on somebody else who was there. Some of them was just stupid, like Susan MacReady telling about the time when Diane thought she had chicken pox even though she'd had it already, but it turned out to be poison ivy.

And some was cruel. Norman Cox did a cruel one, telling that Parker Condon had cheated on his history report, copying most of it out of the encyclopedia, so that Mrs. Hindler spoke to him private and made him do it over. Parker got all tensed up while Norman was telling it. He laughed, pretending like he was tough and didn't care. But we all knew how Parker's parents commanded him to get all A's so's he could go to the same college where his brother was, and how Parker was nervous all the time about it. So it was cruel to tell on him for cheating that wasn't even completely his fault.

After Norman told, Parker yelled out, "Hhhaaaa" and did a fake karate chop across the table at him so's we was all able to start laughing and pretend to forget the cruelness. But I didn't forget. And I thought about a way to get even.

That's why, when it was finally my turn — I was last — I said, "I have one to tell on Norman Cox."

Everybody expected me to say "on Veronica" because Veronica and me has been best friends for so long. So they looked surprised. And Norman sure looked surprised, too.

"On Halloween," I started, trying to make a story out of it the way everybody else had, "me and Veronica took Veronica's little brother out trick-or-treating. He was dressed up like a ballerina, with toe shoes and all."

Everybody started laughing. "*Gunther?*" somebody yelled. "You dressed old Gunther up like a ballerina?"

In the midst of all the laughing and shouting, I saw Veronica's face staring at me. She knew. She knew I was going to tell that Norman hit Millie Bellows in the face with a stone.

I could see she was going to hate me for doing it.

I continued on talking, and I could hear my voice describing how Gunther twirled around, and how he had a magic wand and all. But I was having a whole lot of thoughts at the same time. I was thinking about how Veronica had begun to *like* Norman Cox. And

153

how her liking him had begun to make Norman act different. He was helping at Millie Bellows's house now, and being faithful to it, showing up every time, even though he complained.

I was thinking, too, about what Norman *could* have told, when it was his turn. He could have told about the day he seen Veronica's mother go crazy and try to baptize Gunther in the creek. But he didn't.

I heard myself say, "and while we was hauling old Gunther around in his ballerina costume, we saw Norman Cox and he didn't even know it. And he was wearing his mama's choir robe. Big man Norman Cox was all dressed up like a Presbyterian lady!"

Everybody laughed, and that was it. I didn't say no more. While I watched, Veronica laughed, too, and started in to tease Norman, sitting next to her. Norman put his hands into a praying position and sang, "Rock of Ages, cleeffft for me —" in a high, girly voice.

"AMEN!" we all sang. Then Mrs. Briggs brought in the birthday cake, and pretty soon the party was over.

15

Thanksgiving came, and so did Veronica's grand-parents, all the way from Tennessee. I had met them before, of course, on other visits, but this was the first time we all sat at the same table together, with us girls wearing our new dresses. Her grandmother told stories about when Mr. Bigelow was a little boy Gunther's size. They called him "Flip" then, short for Philip.

Sweet-Ho had cooked a turkey, and me and Veronica had helped to mash up sweet potatoes and put marshmallows on top. Gunther agreed to taste the sweet potatoes, and he did, too; but I noticed that he only ate one bite and then went back to his Chef Boyardee.

Millie Bellows came to our house for Thanksgiving dinner and even commented nicely on everything as if she was taking real pains not to be a grouch on account of it being a holiday and all. She even told about how we was helping her about the house. And

155

she told about Thanksgivings when she was a girl and her brother Howard was still alive, how they used to have little mints at the table, set in paper baskets with Thanksgiving decorations painted on.

Millie Bellows had four helpings of stuffing with gravy on top, and me and Veronica had to hold our napkins to our mouths to keep our laughing down, when she took the fourth.

Grandma Bigelow sang a hymn for us, with the words "Sweet Hosanna" in it, and she taught us so we all sang it with her. Sweet-Ho said she remembered it from when she was a girl but she hadn't heard it since.

We held hands around the table when we said grace.

After dinner, Grandpa Bigelow lit up his pipe, and Millie Bellows fluttered her hands a bit in the air to indicate that the smoke was in her eyes and probably causing her to get cancer, but he didn't notice. Then Millie's head nodded while we was sitting there at the table after dessert, and she fell sound asleep and even snored some.

Veronica told her grandparents about how their names was on her family tree at school, in the form of apples.

"I hope I'm a McIntosh apple," Grandma Bigelow said. "It's my favorite kind. McIntosh makes the best pies."

We all laughed because Grandma Bigelow was somewhat round and pink-colored, like a McIntosh apple; and when we laughed Millie Bellows snorted a

156

bit in her sleep and her eyelids fluttered, but she didn't wake up.

"When Mrs. Hindler gives the family trees back," Veronica said to her grandma, "I'll send you mine in the mail, so you can see your apple."

"School sounds more interesting these days than it was when I was young," Grandpa Bigelow said, puffing on his pipe. "What were your school days like, Sweet Hosanna?"

Sweet-Ho looked somewhat rueful. She stood up and began to collect the dessert plates. "I didn't go very far in school, Mr. Bigelow," she said. "I liked school, but I got married when I was very young."

Veronica's father was looking at her. "Why don't you tell everyone, Sweet-Ho, what you've decided?"

Sweet-Ho stood there for a minute with the plates in her hands. She smiled. "Well, I was going to tell Rabble first. I didn't plan on an announcement or anything. But since it's Thanksgiving, and everybody's here together, and I guess Rabble won't mind if I didn't have a chance to tell her in private —"

"I don't mind," I said, puzzled. "What did you decide?"

Sweet-Ho leaned over and took Millie Bellows's plate, real quiet, so as not to disturb her nap. "I've decided to go to college," she said. "Only at night, so I can still get my work done, of course. But Phil talked to the people at the community college for me, and helped me fill out the application, and — well, it still makes me nervous, thinking about it. But they've said

I can start in the new semester after Christmas. I can study literature."

She stood there, smiling, looking at all of us. "Maybe someday I can be a teacher," she said, kind of shy.

Me and Veronica and Gunther all clapped our hands. "Yaaayyy!" Gunther said, forgetting Millie Bellows's nap. But she didn't wake.

Grandma Bigelow stood up and said, "I declare, if I hadn't drunk all of my coffee, I'd make a toast. You just put those plates right back down on the table, Sweet Hosanna, so I can give you a kiss."

And she did. A big kiss on Sweet-Ho's cheek first, and then one for me, too. "You can be real proud of your mother, Parable," she said.

I was. I am.

Veronica's father helped Grandma and Grandpa Bigelow get their suitcases into the trunk of the car the day after Thanksgiving. They was going on from Highriver to Baltimore to visit a niece.

Grandpa Bigelow was leaning over the kitchen table where he had a map all spread out. He was following the road with his finger, peering at it through his glasses. "Look at this, Parable," he said. "She wants to take this scenic route through the mountains. But you look here, now, how much shorter it would be if we just went on the interstate like normal folk."

Well, he was right, of course. Anybody could see that. But I kind of liked the way them little roads

158

curled through the mountains. One of them went real close to Collyer's Run, where I lived with Gnomie when I was a little girl.

"See this here?" I told him. I pointed with my fingertip. "Right here is where Sweet-Ho was born, and where I lived when I was little."

"Is that a fact?"

I nodded. "It surely is pretty there. Even this time of year, when the trees is mostly bare. I bet anything you'd see deer if you went that way."

"Antique shops, too, I suppose. She always wants to go where the antique shops are," he said in a gruff voice, pretending it made him mad.

"I expect you're right. There's antique shops. When Gnomie — that's my grandma — died, somebody came and bought some of her old stuff. We didn't even know it would be worth money. Some quilts, and a table, and some of her kitchen stuff she'd always had, and nobody in the family wanted it, it was all so old-fashioned. So I expect it ended up in an antique shop."

He folded up the map. "Well, I'll humor her and go the scenic route, on your advice, Parable. Where do you suppose she's gone to now? We'll never get on the road at this rate."

We found Grandma Bigelow in the living room with her tape measure out, measuring skinny old Gunther so's she could knit him a sweater. None of us told her that he was allergic to wool, and even Gunther was polite and said he wanted a blue one.

Grandpa Bigelow gave Veronica and me each a five-dollar bill, and a crisp new dollar to Gunther. We all hugged goodbye.

"You give Alice our love, Philip," I heard Grandma Bigelow say to Veronica's daddy, and he nodded his head. Then they were gone.

Mr. Bigelow went every Saturday to Meadowhill. Every Saturday when he came back, he said that Veronica's mother was a little better. I always smiled and said, "That's nice," and so did Sweet-Ho. But it got so's it was just something we said with no meaning, something like you might say politely to the mailman, and two minutes later you would forget you even said it. She's a little better. That's nice. She seems better. That's nice. Somewhat better. That's nice.

It got much colder, and Norman Cox put salt on the steps and front walk at Millie Bellows's house, where sometimes it was icy in the morning. Millie didn't go out none, though, not in the cold. She sat huddled up in front of her TV, watching game shows, drinking tea, and dozing off. Mr. Bigelow checked her furnace now and again to be sure there was always plenty of oil, and Sweet-Ho brought her groceries a couple of times a week.

We invited her for Christmas dinner, but she said no, she wasn't feeling real good. So it was just us, just our family, at Christmas. Gunther played like he believed in Santa Claus even though he'd spied his train set in its box on the hall closet shelf the week before.

So when Veronica and me opened up our biggest boxes and found velveteen bathrobes, we pretended that Mrs. Santa Claus had stitched them up on her sewing machine, and we said we was amazed that she even got our sizes just right.

We decorated the whole downstairs, with popcorn strings and holly and pine boughs on the mantelpiece. Veronica hung mistletoe from the ceiling light in the hall, and we all grabbed Gunther and gave him big juicy kisses every time he walked through. After a while we noticed that he was hanging about the hall a whole lot, just waiting and hoping.

Christmas night me and Veronica went to bed early because we both had got new books and we wanted to curl up in our beds to read. My book was called *The Yearling,* and lord, when I opened it up and began to read I found that it had another Jody, same as *The Red Pony.* But this Jody was different. He lived with his mama and daddy in a place that was all woods and swamps, and when I read I felt as if I was right there, too, where it was quiet but for birds and growing things. I began to see Jody's home as being somewhat like Gnomie's, not fancy or nothing, but so filled up with hard work and hopes and haves and haven'ts all tangled there together in ways that tugged and ached.

I was in my new green bathrobe — it was as soft as the moss that grows down by the creek in summer — and after a while I marked my place in the book and got up to go brush my teeth. In the hall, all of a sudden, I felt an urge to go and peer over the stair railing, just to look one more time at the decorations and the lights on the tree, just to see it again while it was still Christmas, before the time was past. Each year it goes by too quick, and you got to try to make it last however which way you can. My way was to take one more look before I went to sleep.

So I tiptoed over to the place where you can stand against the upstairs railing and look down the curving stairs and beyond, into the hall and through the archway into the living room.

There was only the light of the fireplace, the Christmas candles in each window, and the lights on the tree. There was the sound of Christmas music coming from the radio. And there was the smell of pine.

Then I seen something that was supposed to be private. I didn't mean to. I only wanted to make the feeling of Christmas last for one more long look that I could store in my memory.

But then I had this, to store in my memory, too, and it was so private that I knew I couldn't even tell Veronica, though I had always told her everything. Mr. Bigelow and Sweet-Ho, while I watched, they was standing there beside the Christmas tree, and he was fixing one of the little lights. Then he turned around to her — she was laughing in her low voice — and all of a sudden she was quiet, and they kissed for a long time.

16

Millie Bellows died the day of Sweet-Ho's first exam.

Me and Veronica found her, huddled there in her afghan with a cup of tea on the table not even touched. We thought she was asleep, same as usual. The TV was blaring. It was the middle of *The Newlywed Game*. The guy was asking all the wives: "What farm animal best describes your husband on your wedding night — a stallion, a chicken, or a jackass?" and all the wives were giggling while they tried to answer.

"Mrs. Bellows," I said in a loud voice, "that's downright trashy, and you should switch channels."

She didn't move or look up, and then I realized. Her eyes was partly open, with her glasses tipped a little crooked, and one hand was just dangling down beside the chair. I knew she was dead. I picked up her hand real gentle to put it back in her lap, and it was cold.

Veronica started in trembling and she backed away.

"It's nothing to be scared of, Veronica," I told her. "Turn the TV off and then call your daddy on the phone."

I sat beside Millie while Veronica did those things. I wondered should I do something else, maybe try to lay her down and close her eyes. But I just sat and patted the cold hand.

"Now call Norman," I said, after Veronica told her daddy and he said he would come right away. "Because he's supposed to come over and start working on fixing that loose cellar step. But there's no need for everybody in the world to be here now. Millie wouldn't like it any."

When she had done that, I said, "Now make some tea."

"What for?" Veronica asked. Her voice was still shaky. "She can't —"

"Of course she can't. She's dead as a doornail," I told her. "Make some for you and me."

Mr. Bigelow got there in no time, and he hugged Veronica and me. He said we could go home, and he would take care of everything else.

Before we left Millie's house, I asked Mr. Bigelow something. I asked him if Veronica and me could take a souvenir to keep.

He hesitated. "Did you have something special in mind?" he asked.

I pulled out the old photograph album, the one we had looked at so many times with Millie Bellows.

"Just a photograph," I said. "Could we each have one, from when she was a girl?"

He looked at the little stacks of photographs stuck in every which way between the pages. He nodded his head. "One each," he said. "She wouldn't mind."

So we each chose one. It seemed odd to be turning the pages of the album without her grabbing at our arms and interrupting to say what each thing was, to tell about all the people in her past. I chose one of her all alone, with a big bow in her hair, when she was staring straight into the camera with solemn eyes. She was just my age in that one, and not knowing at all what her future would be, any more than I know mine right now.

Veronica cried some on the way home, and I don't fault her none for that. But I didn't cry. I felt sorry that Millie's old age wasn't real pleasant, and there was times when I liked her okay, and even sometimes when I liked her a whole lot if she forgot her crabbiness and talked about old times. But I didn't love Millie Bellows.

We found Sweet-Ho in the kitchen with her college books all spread out around her on the table. She'd been worrying all week about her very first test, and we'd all been teasing her, Mr. Bigelow and Veronica and me, and even Gunther some, though Gunther didn't understand about college.

When we came through the back door, she looked up and smiled. "You're home early," she said.

"Millie Bellows is dead," I told her. "She died watching game shows, and Mr. Bigelow is taking care

165

of everything, and don't you dare stay home from school and miss that exam or I'll never forgive you, ever."

Then Sweet-Ho cried some, too. But that night, after supper, she put on her coat and grabbed up her books and went and took the exam, her first one ever since she was thirteen years old. And she got the second highest grade in the class.

Not many people came to Millie's funeral. We were there, of course, and some of the other neighbors, and a nephew from Parkersburg. Mrs. Cox was there with Norman, and Mr. Cox did the service, telling some about Millie's long life and about how helpful she was in the neighborhood, some of which was a lie. But I did think back on the melty Jell-O she brought over the day Mrs. Bigelow went crazy. She *meant* to be helpful sometimes.

It was a cold, murky day, with a gray sky smudged like a chalky blackboard. When we left the church — there was no cemetery to go to, because her nephew was taking her to Parkersburg to be buried there — I marched right over to where Norman Cox was standing with his mother and I asked him could I speak to him private.

He looked some surprised, but he followed me where I led him, over to the edge of the parking lot where there was an icy old mud puddle with a piece of newspaper frozen into it.

"You probably don't even remember that Millie

Bellows's brother Howard died when he was fourteen years old because he acted stupid and show-offy, and she felt bad about it all her life," I told him.

"So?" Norman said. "So what?"

"So here," I said. "I'm going to give you this."

I took the mashed-up old choir hat out of my coat pocket and handed it to him. He took it, but he looked at it like he didn't know what it was.

"It's the hat you was wearing Halloween night, when you acted stupid and show-offy and chunked the stone that blacked Millie Bellows's eye," I said.

"I didn't mean to hit her," Norman muttered. "I was only —"

"I know," I interrupted. "You was only trying to call attention to yourself. But it was stupid and show-offy."

Norman stuffed the hat into the pocket of his jacket. He didn't even look at me. He didn't say nothing. I didn't expect him to.

"By the time she died, she thought you was a nice boy. She told me and Veronica so," I said. "I was just thinking that probably she never got around to telling you."

He still didn't say nothing.

"So I'm telling you on her behalf," I said. "The newspaper said she was ninety-three years old. I hope you don't ever forget that once you blacked the eye of a ninety-three-year-old lady. But at least I think you ought to know she never realized it was you who done it, and before she died she said you were a nice young man.

"That's all I wanted to say," I told him, and I walked away.

Just before our February school vacation Mrs. Hindler took down the family trees from the classroom wall and gave them back to us. The colors in them had begun to fade, hanging there in the sunshine all those months, though there was a small new brighter spot on Corrine Foster's where just after Thanksgiving she had climbed on a chair to paste up a new apple for her newborn baby sister. "Sarah Hope," it said, "born November 29."

I stood mine up on my dresser, right next to Millie Bellows's girlhood picture.

"Sometimes I remember Millie Bellows with a kind of fondness," I told Sweet-Ho one night while I was getting ready for bed. "But I really *love* my memories of Gnomie."

"Me too," Sweet-Ho said. "When I think of her I always think of the smell of cinnamon cookies."

"I think of big blue delphiniums."

"And her aprons. I remember the aprons, all starched and ironed."

"Once," I said, "when I was little, there was a big rainstorm at night. Gnomie and me was watching it through the window. And then she got the idea to go outside and stand right in it. So we did that, laughing and laughing. The wind was blowing the trees every which way, and our nightgowns, too. When we came in she dried my hair in front of the wood stove."

168

Sweet-Ho smiled. "Sometimes I miss all of that, just a little."

"Me too, I guess. But it doesn't make me sad, because I love our life now. Anyways, I expect it wouldn't be the same if we was to go back, not with Gnomie gone."

"And not with us so different now," Sweet-Ho said.

"Are we? Are we different now?"

"Of course. Nobody stays the same."

"Especially not *you*, Sweet-Ho. Shoot, you're a college student now! Isn't that the most amazing thing?"

"It surely is," Sweet-Ho said. "And I'd better go and get some studying done. You get to sleep, Rabble. Dream of wind and rain."

"I will," I told her, as I snuggled down. "If I set my mind to it, I can dream anything I want."

17

One evening Veronica's father said that it was time, next Saturday, for Veronica to go with him to Meadowhill again, and that this time Gunther was to go, too.

Veronica didn't say nothing, but old agreeable Gunther, he looked up and said, "Sure thing!" Then he hiccuped and grinned. He didn't know nothing about Meadowhill, what it was, what it meant.

Saturday afternoon me and Sweet-Ho went off together to the movies. We ate popcorn and ice cream sandwiches and laughed at a dumb old comedy, and we didn't talk, neither one of us, about Meadowhill at all.

They got back late in the afternoon, and that night me and Veronica took a walk after supper, all bundled up against the cold. We walked over to where Millie Bellows's house stood empty. In the spring they was to paint it and sell it.

"They'll have to cut all them old vines down before they paint," I said.

"They'll grow back good as new. I hope they paint it gold."

"I hope white," I said, just to be ornery. Something inside me was making me feel fretful.

"Well, white would be nice, too. When the yard is all cleaned up, it'll be pretty. By next summer maybe there'll be a new family living here. I wonder if they'll have kids."

"I hope not," I said, knowing I was acting just as grouchy as Millie Bellows used to. "There's enough kids in this neighborhood."

Veronica started in to laugh. "Rabble, that's silly! There's only you and me and Gunther and Norman! And before long, you and me and Norman won't even be kids, we're all growing up so fast."

"How's your mother?" I asked all of a sudden. Not knowing about the afternoon at Meadowhill was what was making me so crabby.

"She's getting well," Veronica said. She leaned down and picked up a broken shingle from Millie Bellows's yard, where it had fallen from the roof.

"How can you even tell, if she don't talk any, or even comb her hair?"

Veronica looked startled. "Rabble, that was way back in the fall when she didn't comb her hair! That was months ago! This afternoon she looked just as pretty as anything, and she talked a whole lot. She sat with Gunther on her lap and we talked about all sorts of things, all four of us."

"Well, shoot," I said, "what do you expect? Somebody holds somebody else under water forever and practically drowns them, of *course* they're going to try all sorts of ways to make amends. Of *course* they're going to try to act normal."

Veronica dropped the shingle back on the ground. She looked at me real steady. "She wasn't acting, Rabble. She's really getting better."

"I'm going back," I said, and turned away. "I have to help Sweet-Ho with her typing tonight. She can do forty words a minute now when I read something to her.

"My mother is making amazing progress with her studies," I added, with my back to Veronica. "I surely am astounded that you haven't commented on it." I walked away.

Back home, in the kitchen, I was already dictating stuff to Sweet-Ho when Veronica came through the back door. Mr. Bigelow had brought home an old typewriter from his office and Sweet-Ho was learning to type so's she could write her term papers and such properly. She practiced every night at a table in the corner of the kitchen. Sometimes she let me practice too, though I wasn't much good and went real slow with lots of mistakes.

"Shoot," Sweet-Ho said, and stopped typing. "I missed the *q* again. I wish they didn't have the *q*'s in the alphabet. There doesn't seem much need of them."

"Sure there is," Veronica said, pulling off her coat.

"Listen: I think it's quite, quite, quite wonderful that you're doing so well, so quickly, in school, Sweet-Ho. Hear all the *q*'s?"

Sweet-Ho laughed. "I do. Thank you, Veronica."

"How about if I make us some hot chocolate, Veronica?" I asked. "It was cold out."

"Thanks," Veronica said, and I knew we was friends again.

But things were changing. Now Veronica and Gunther went every Saturday, with their daddy, to Meadowhill. Gunther began to talk about his mama at home.

One afternoon he was fooling around with his toys on the floor, and suddenly he said, "My mama will be coming home soon."

Sweet-Ho looked up from where she was sitting with a book, but she didn't say nothing. Veronica looked up, too, but she didn't say nothing either.

I did. I said, "Big Gun, your mama was sick for a long time. Four whole years, maybe even longer, before it started to show."

Gunther just grinned. "Uh-huh," he said. He didn't even know what I was talking about, but good old Gunther, he just agreed with everybody.

"So," I went on, "even though it's real nice that she's getting better, still and all it'll take a long time for her to be entirely well again."

Gunther smiled happily and ran his truck around, under the legs of a chair.

"Probably four years at least," I said. "Maybe even five or six."

Veronica said, "That's not true, Rabble. Really. She's getting well real fast now."

"I just don't want him to get his hopes up high, Veronica," I explained to her, "because there are always setbacks, you know."

Gunther hadn't even been listening to me, I guess, because that night at dinner he said it again, when his daddy was there. "My mama's coming home soon," he said. "Isn't that right, Daddy?"

Mr. Bigelow was busy handing round the plates. "Could be, Big Gun," he said. I was sure glad that he made it uncertain that way so that old Gunther's hopes wouldn't be too high. I said so, later, to Sweet-Ho when we was alone.

"Don't you think Mr. Bigelow's wise in the way he answers Gunther? Not getting up his hopes and all, about Mrs. Bigelow coming home soon?"

We was up in our room while Sweet-Ho gathered up her school things because she was about to go to class. "Phil told me that they hope for June, Rabble. They hope she'll come home in June."

"June? But it's already March! June's only three months away!"

"That's right," Sweet-Ho said, busying herself with her pens and all.

"But, Sweet-Ho! What're we going to do, you and me?"

She looked over at me. "Me, I'm going to be typing sixty words a minute by June, and I'm going to get

174

an A in American Literature, that's what I'm going to do. You — well, I hope you're going to get out your Geography book and do your homework this minute."

I glared at her. "That's not what I meant."

She softened her look. "I know it wasn't, honey," she said. "But right now it's the only answer I've got."

When she had gone, I wandered down to Veronica's room and found her sprawled on her bed with her own Geography book.

"I hate Uruguay," she said when I went in. "It's too hard."

"Me too," I told her. "I'm just bored silly by South America. I can't spell any part of it except Peru."

"You want to play cards or something instead of homework? Daddy wouldn't know. He's watching TV."

I shook my head. "Veronica," I said, "I got to speak to you about something serious. I got to tell you that Sweet-Ho said your mother's probably coming home in June —"

"I know," she said. "Daddy told me."

"Well," I said, "I'm scared about that."

"Me too."

I was surprised. "You are? But I thought you was glad."

"Were. 'I thought you *were* glad.'"

"Okay, were. But don't correct me now, Veronica. Talk to me about being scared."

Veronica fiddled with the pages in her notebook. "I *am* glad. But I'm scared because what if she gets sick again? What if she doesn't remember to take her med-

175

icine? Daddy says she won't, but I keep thinking what if —"

"What about me and Sweet-Ho, Veronica? That's what *I'm* scared of!"

"What do you mean?"

I looked down at her bedspread and plucked at the little bumpy parts that made a pattern in it. "I can't go back and live in a garage again, Veronica. I just can't. Not after being a family altogether. Not after us being like sisters all this time."

"That won't change, Rabble. You can still live here. It'll be just the same."

I looked up. "It will? Are you sure?"

She giggled. "Cross my heart and hope to die, stick a needle in my eye," she said, like we used to when we was little kids.

But later, when I lay in bed, with Uruguay all closed up on the floor beside me, I began to see it all in my head and I knew that Veronica was wrong. What I saw was our whole family with somebody added to it. That somebody was Veronica's mother. I saw her sitting there at the dinner table, in the chair where Sweet-Ho was accustomed to sitting. I saw her in the living room on the couch beside Veronica's daddy, while he would be reading out loud from a book, maybe *The Red Pony*, and I couldn't see where Sweet-Ho would be, or how she would look. I couldn't feel how Sweet-Ho would feel.

Outside, against the window, I could hear the oak tree — the one we called the Family Tree — brush against the window in the breeze. Its leaves would be

176

coming back soon, with spring. Each spring it was the same, but changed, like every family tree, with things dropped off, things added. Millie Bellows: we had pictured her perched up there, quarrelsome as always. Now she was gone. Norman Cox: he wouldn't be up in that tree the way we had pretended, zinging stones and paper clips no more. That Norman Cox was gone, and in his place was someone nicer, someone more grown up. And Mrs. Bigelow: we had laughed, thinking of her sitting up there in her gauzy dress, calling out baptisms. She had been gone, and now she'd be back, but different, maybe a real mother again. And me and Sweet-Ho, we were different, too.

Veronica said it would be the same for us all, in the Bigelows' house. But I knew she was wrong. I remembered the private thing I had never told nobody, the night that I stood in the hall looking down, and saw Sweet-Ho kiss Veronica's father. I knew that that one night had made everything different, had made it so that things would have to change.

It scared me, knowing.

18

One Saturday morning at the end of April I woke up and heard birds singing so loud that I looked out the window to see if maybe there were five thousand of them in the yard all of a sudden, like in that old movie on TV, the scary one that you don't want to watch all alone.

But this wasn't scary. It was just noisy, all that singing and chirping. It had rained some, in the night. Now the sun was shining, and the yard was full of spring.

The whole world seemed changed. There were flowers coming up everywhere, the tips of daffodils and hyacinths bursting from the ground. The grass was green, the air was warm, and the trees were weighted with wet shiny buds the color of limes.

Down in the kitchen, Sweet-Ho was singing, too, and I could hear Gunther scampering about, maybe even dancing, for all I knew. Gunther was that sort, the sort that might dance if he felt like it, and not even caring that he might look foolish.

From my window I could see Norman Cox come along on his bike, skittering pebbles from his rear tire, same as always. No jacket, no hat, just his old jeans and T-shirt, and his big feet in those crummy old sneakers. He skidded to a stop right below our windows and put down one foot to balance hisself.

"Veronica? Rabble? You up?" he yelled, and when I poked my head out the window I could look over and see Veronica's head poke out of hers, too.

"Come on down!" Norman called. "Somebody's moving into Millie Bellows's house today!"

I knew that the house had been sold because Mr. Bigelow had told us. It was freshly painted — dark gray, with shiny new black shutters at each window — and the vines were trimmed, the lawn mowed, the plumbing fixed, and the floors polished. Millie Bellows's nephew had sold it to a family that was moving to Highriver all the way from Vermont. The father was going to teach at the college, the mother had red hair, and there was a little kid. That's all Mr. Bigelow knew.

Me and Veronica and Norman — no, wait. Veronica and Norman and I (I'm working on my grammar) headed on over just in time to see the Mayflower guys start to unload the van. Norman parked his bike against a tree and we all stood there at the edge of the lawn, watching. It gives you a funny feeling to see somebody's furniture standing about in a yard, and being carried into a house, as if you're spying on something private. Like you don't have no right — no, wait. Like you *haven't any* right to know that they own a yellow couch and a Posturepedic mattress since they haven't *invited* you to know those things. But there it all is, offered up for viewing.

After a while a station wagon with a Vermont license plate and a CHILD ON BOARD sticker drove up, and there were our new neighbors: a woman with red hair, a man, and a little kid, just like Mr. Bigelow said. The woman lifted the kid out of a car seat and I could see he was just the size of Gunther, though better-looking, with more meat on his bones, and curly red-blond hair. He was wearing a shirt with a picture of Winnie-the-Pooh, and he was grouchy as all get-out, whining and rubbing his eyes. I expect he had been asleep so I didn't fault him any for the grouchiness. He blinked his eyes, looking around, and spied us standing there.

"It's okay, Johnny," I heard his mother say. "Go on over and say hello." She smiled at us.

So the little kid wandered over to where we were. Veronica knelt down and tied one of his sneakers, which was dragging its laces. "Hi," she said.

He rubbed his eyes again. His cheek had a zigzag wrinkle on it, all pressed in from where his head had been laying while he slept. "Hi," he said, and yawned.

"How old are you?" Veronica asked.

He thought, and then he held up one hand with his thumb tucked in and four fingers sticking up.

180

"Four?" Veronica asked, and he nodded sleepily.

"I have a brother four years old," she told him. "His name is Gunther."

"Here comes Gunther now," Norman said, looking over toward our house. And sure enough, here came Gunther, trotting through the yard, with *his* sneakers untied, too. Next thing we knew, Gunther and Johnny were running about together, saying silly four-year-old things to each other and getting in the way of the moving men so that the lady — she told us her name was Mrs. Elliot — had to remind them now and then to watch out. But she said it real nice, and smiling the whole time; you could tell she was pleased that her little boy had a friend right off, their first day here.

All the while the furniture was going in, and some porch stuff, chairs and a settee, were left on the porch, so that the house was taking on the look of a new family, and the feeling of Millie Bellows was disappearing like wind blowing away. So that was another way the world had changed.

Norman offered to help with some small stuff, lifting boxes that had been piled in the yard, taking the ones marked "Tools" to the shed out back, and telling the Elliots some things about the house: how the shed door needed tightening up, how the cherry tree ought to be pruned and sprayed so they could get some good cherries off it next summer. Norman Cox, smiling, being pleasant and helpful — that was one more change that had come on gradual-like, so that suddenly in the spring you could see it full-blown, same

181

as a daffodil bulb coming up in the yard, and it took you by surprise because you forgot that you had planted it there.

Before a week passed, old Gunther and Johnny was — no, wait — *were* best friends, off together prowling about the neighborhood. Next thing we knew, a couple of weeks later, they both of them had poison ivy something fierce, from playing back at the edge of Millie Bellows's old yard where the brush needed to be cleared. They were both of them smeared head to toe with calamine lotion and itching to beat the band. Gunther was some delighted about that. "I never knew anybody else who itched," he said, with a look of surprise. I thought to myself that there are all sorts of reasons for friendships and itching might be just as good as any of the rest of them.

Mrs. Hindler singled me out in the classroom one day, calling attention to the way my grammar had improved. She did it in a nice way so I didn't feel embarrassed or nothing — no, wait — or *anything* is what I meant. She just said to me and to the whole class, in a friendly way, that it proved you could do anything you set your mind to.

And that was true, because I *had* set my mind to it, to talking right, to making Sweet-Ho and all the Bigelows proud. Parker Condon had even told me that he hoped we could go to the same college, and I acted agreeable and polite, though I didn't have my heart set on it the way he seemed to.

Sometimes, though, I missed my old way of talking. It was because my Gnomie had talked in a country way, and when I left off talking like Gnomie, I felt as if she was disappearing, same as Millie Bellows when her house was changed.

But Sweet-Ho, when I told her that, said, "Rabble, I expect wherever she is, your Gnomie's looking down and feeling downright contented to see you growing up so educated."

"You too," I pointed out.

Sweet-Ho laughed. "I expect she'd *faint* to see me!" she said.

Sweet-Ho had just finished her final exams, and school was ending for me, too, when Mr. Bigelow took his pen one night and drew a circle around the twenty-first on the calendar page for June. He told us that on that day he would be bringing Veronica's mother home. A nurse would come with her, and stay for a while, but that didn't worry me. There was still the little apartment over the garage, where the nurse could stay, I figured.

That night, and the next, he and Sweet-Ho stayed up late, talking and talking. I could hear their voices from my bed, and sometimes it seemed as if they were arguing. But I never sneaked to the railing to listen. I knew that it was theirs to decide, and that it wouldn't be easy, and that when the deciding was done, Sweet-Ho would tell me.

Still, when she did, I wasn't ready to hear what she had to say.

We were alone in the house on a Saturday afternoon when Veronica and Gunther and their daddy had gone to Meadowhill.

"I want to show you something, Rabble," Sweet-Ho said. She took some papers from her desk. I could see where she had typed in her name, SWEET HOSANNA STARKEY, at the top, after the place where it said "Name" and left a space.

"What's that?" I asked her.

"It's my application blank for college next year," she said. "I'm going to be going full-time. They've already told me they'll accept me, but I have to send the forms in by next week."

"But who'll — " I interrupted myself and laughed. "I started to say, 'Who'll look after Gunther?' but I forgot that of course his mama will be home. And Veronica and I can help, too."

"No, Rabble, it won't be that way," Sweet-Ho said, and held the paper out to me. "Look. This isn't Highriver Community College. This is the Clarksburg branch of the university."

"I don't understand." I took the paper and held it, reading her name again, and all the other things she had filled in. "How can you go to Clarksburg? That's eighty miles away."

"Rabble," she said, "I don't want to be a babysitter and a housekeeper all my life. I want to be a teacher. I can't do that by just taking courses here at night. So I'm going to be a real, honest-to-goodness student at the university. I've been saving most of my pay for four years now, and I can afford the tuition. I've figured and figured, and it won't be easy, but I can do it. I know I can."

"Sweet-Ho, you can't drive that far every day. Not in the winter, when the weather's bad. I just don't see how —"

"Listen to me, Rabble, honey. This is hard for you, I know, but I want you to listen. We have an apartment in Clarksburg. You and me, starting June fifteenth. Phil is giving me the old car — I've promised to pay him back someday, when I can — and he helped me find a job in a real estate office there, so I can work part time and afford our rent. It's going to be tough, Rabble, working and going to school, but you know I'm not afraid of hard work. I never have been before and I won't be now."

"You mean we're leaving here?" I was only just beginning to understand. "Is Mr. Bigelow making us go away?"

"No. *I've* decided to go away."

I turned on her in anger. "You can't do that! This is our home! This is our family!"

But Sweet-Ho shook her head. "You and me, Rabble, *we* are our family. Not the Bigelows. Now that their family's back together, it's time for you and me to move on." She took the papers back from me, folded them, and put them on her desk.

I argued. "We don't take up much room! Just the guest room is all, and we keep it tidy and picked up! And what'll Veronica say? She won't be able to *bear* it, Sweet-Ho! I'm her very best friend! Veronica and me are like sisters!"

I started to cry. But even when I was talking, arguing, crying, I knew it was decided and that it wouldn't change. And you know the strangest thing? The strangest thing was that deep down, I knew Sweet-Ho had made the right choice. The choice to move on.

It was hard to pack. Not because we had so much, but because we had so little. Each thing Sweet-Ho and I owned was special, and so with each folding, with each wrapping, with each placing in a box, came memories that we had to talk about.

I packed a going-away present Parker Condon had given me, a nice little book to write in. It had flowers on the cover and said "My Travels" in gold letters. Inside, he had written, "To Parable Starkey. From your friend, Parker Condon." I was glad he hadn't written "Love," because even though I had tried to pretend a little, I just couldn't love someone with spiky hair like his.

One night, when I was putting the things from my dresser into a cardboard box, I came upon the composition I wrote for school at the beginning of the year.

"My Home," it was called. I read it again, to myself, and laughed a little. Parts of it sounded funny now.

"Sweet-Ho," I said, and she looked over from where she was taking things from the closet.

"What?" she asked.

"I have to take some time off from packing, to write something," I told her.

"That's all right. There's no rush. We'll have it all ready by Friday."

So I took my notebook and pen and rewrote the composition. This time I didn't even need the thesaurus, and it was a good thing, too, because it was already packed away in the box marked "Books."

This time I wrote:

MY HOME

My home has many things in it that I love. It has a dictionary and a thesaurus; patchwork quilts made by my grandmother, who passed away a long time ago when I was just a little girl; a funny bear-shaped cookie jar; a pillow filled with pine needles, which remind me of the smell of the woods behind the house where I lived when I was twelve;

I stopped for a minute, holding the pen. "Sweet-Ho," I asked, "do we have to take that old toaster? It never worked right. It always burned the toast."

"I'm going to give it to the church for the rummage sale," she said. "Let someone else eat burnt toast. We'll save up and get a new one."

I wrote some more.

and a pale blue glass vase, which holds flowers
all summer long.

I stopped again. "Sweet-Ho," I asked, "do you think
I'll ever see Veronica again?"
She nodded. "I'm sure you will."

The best friends I have throughout my life
will always be welcome in my home, even if I
haven't seen them for a very long time.

At night, in my home, I can listen and hear
the things outside: birds and wind and rain. Inside, at night, after I am in bed, sometimes I
can hear my mother singing in a low voice. She
knows a hymn from her own childhood, a
hymn her own mother used to sing, and it says
her name: Sweet Hosanna.

All of these things together give my home
the good feelings that it has. No matter where a
home might be, feelings are the vital thing.

"There," I said, and closed my notebook. "It feels
good to fix something up so it's right."

On Friday morning, early, the car was packed and it
was time to drive away. I cried, and so did Sweet-Ho.
Veronica sobbed and sobbed, and I believe I could see
some tears in Mr. Bigelow's eyes. Not Gunther,
though. He just hiccuped and grinned. Good old
Gunther, he always expected that things would turn
out okay no matter what, and when your expectations
are like Gunther's, then there's no need to cry ever.

188

I think that the reason he cried so much when he was first born was because his expectations were so measly then.

I hugged and kissed him goodbye and got exposed to ringworm, impetigo, and poison ivy all in one swoop, and didn't even care.

As we drove out of Highriver, along the highway, I looked up and saw the Rockwell house sitting there on its hilltop. "I'm going to write to Veronica every single day," I told Sweet-Ho. "We have lots of plans for the future so we have to keep in touch.

"What about you?" I asked her. "Are you going to write to Mr. Bigelow?"

She smiled. "I surely will let him know now and then how we're doing," she said, "because he did so much to help us along. But I expect I'll be awful busy. I won't have time to write letters much."

"I know you love him," I said suddenly, looking at her sideways as she drove.

"I loved all the Bigelows and always will," Sweet-Ho said.

That was true, I knew, but I wanted more from her. I wanted to know how you could bear to go away from someone you love. How you could *choose* it.

"But, Sweet-Ho, I know you loved him special," I said. "More special even than Gunther."

She didn't turn her head or blink her eyes, and she talked steady and strong, looking down the road that wound ahead of us all the way to Clarksburg. "There are lots of different kinds of love," she said. "You know that."

"I surely do. From my thesaurus." I started reciting some. "Affection. Passion. Regard. All sorts of kinds."

Sweet-Ho smiled. "And they get mixed up together sometimes, so you can't tell which is which. And you know what? Some of them are just pretend."

I thought about that. "For a while," I told her, "I pretended that I loved Parker Condon. But I didn't really."

"Well, you'll understand, then. For a little while I think I pretended that I loved Mr. Bigelow in a way that I didn't, not really. And maybe he pretended, too."

I nodded. "I expect the one he *really* loves is Veronica and Gunther's mother. I hope she's really all better."

"I hope so, too."

"And you know what I hope for you, Sweet-Ho? I hope you find the one *you* really love. Besides me, of course."

"I will, someday. We both will. Because we're moving on to where more things are in store."

I kept silent for a minute, thinking about what she said. Then I twisted around and looked into the back seat, at the carton filled with books where it lay under our folded quilts.

"Remember those two books, Sweet-Ho?" I asked her. "My very favorite ones — *The Red Pony* and *The Yearling*? Both of them with a boy named Jody?"

She nodded, watching the road.

"I'm just now realizing that they're both about the

190

same thing. About all kinds of loving, and about saying goodbye. And about moving on to where more things are in store."

"They're about growing older," Sweet-Ho said.

"And growing up."

I sighed and slouched down in my seat, fiddling with the seat belt and then leaning over to mess with the radio dial. Then I leaned back and watched the road along with Sweet-Ho. I watched the river pass by on the right, the fields all stretched out beside us, the woods here and there, and the West Virginia mountains beyond.

"You know what I'm thinking, Sweet-Ho?" I asked.

"Of course I don't," she said. "You tell me."

"I'm thinking that up ahead, up there where the road curves around by those trees, any minute now we might come around that curve, and there beside the road we might be downright amazed to see a blue pickup truck parked, waiting. And sitting there in it will be the handsomest man you ever saw, and he'll have ginger-colored hair."

Sweet-Ho threw back her head and laughed and laughed. "Parable Ann Starkey, if that happens, you just hold onto your hat and keep an eye out for the state police. Because if that happens, I'm going to press my foot down hard on this gas pedal and sail on past. You and me, Rabble, we've got too much waiting for us up ahead."

She sped up a little, driving real careful, and when we went around the curve I looked, and it was all a blur. But there was nothing there. There was only Sweet Hosanna and me, and outside the whole world, quiet in the early morning, green and strewn with brand new blossoms, like the ones on my very best dress.

Rabble Starkey

By: Lowry, Lois
Quiz No. 5035
BL 5.3   IL MG

Word	GL
ambition	6
fondness	6
homely	6
observed	5
peered	5
recital	7
shuffling	5
solemn	8
sorrow	5
vital	7